DISNEY
MINNIE MOUSE

THE PERFECT BOOK

A GRAPHIC NOVEL

by Brooke Vitale

graphix
An Imprint of
SCHOLASTIC

All rights reserved. Published by Graphix, an imprint of Scholastic Inc.,
Publishers since 1920. SCHOLASTIC, GRAPHIX, and associated logos are trademarks
and/or registered trademarks of Scholastic Inc.

The publisher does not have any control over and does not assume any responsibility for
author or third-party websites or their content.

ISBN 978-1-338-74331-9

10 9 8 7 6 5 4 3 2 1   21 22 23 24 25

Printed in the U.S.A. 40

First edition, October 2021
Written by Brooke Vitale
Illustrated by Artful Doodlers, Ltd.
Book design by Jeff Shake

PART 1

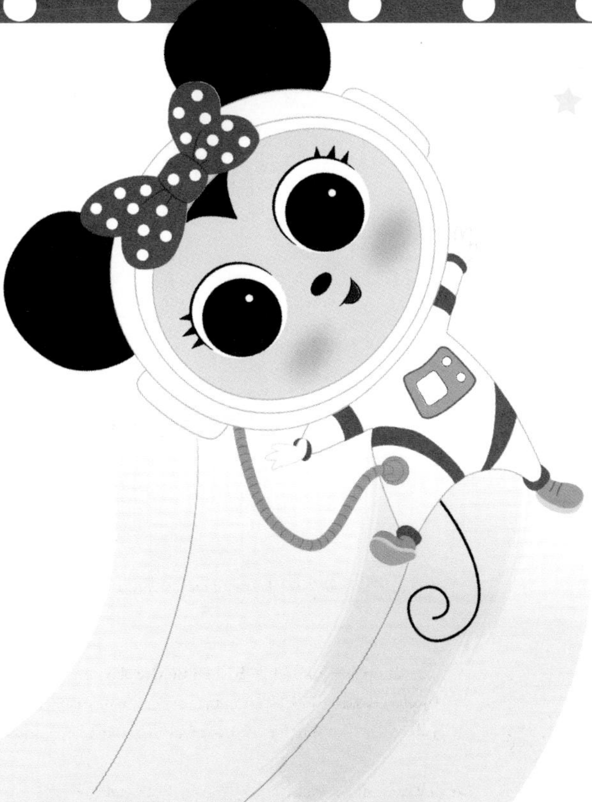

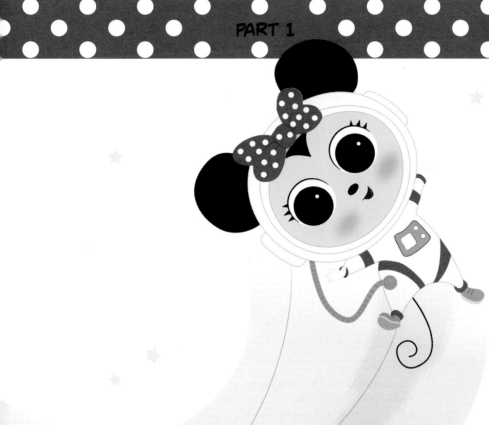

ASTRONAUT MINNIE TO THE RESCUE

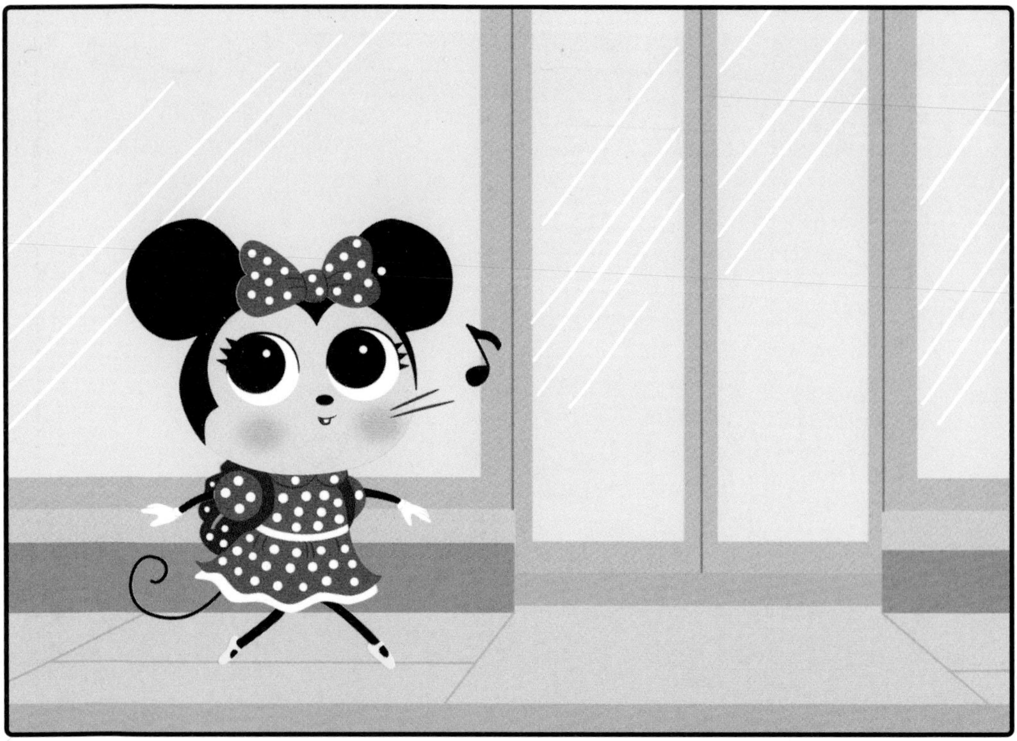

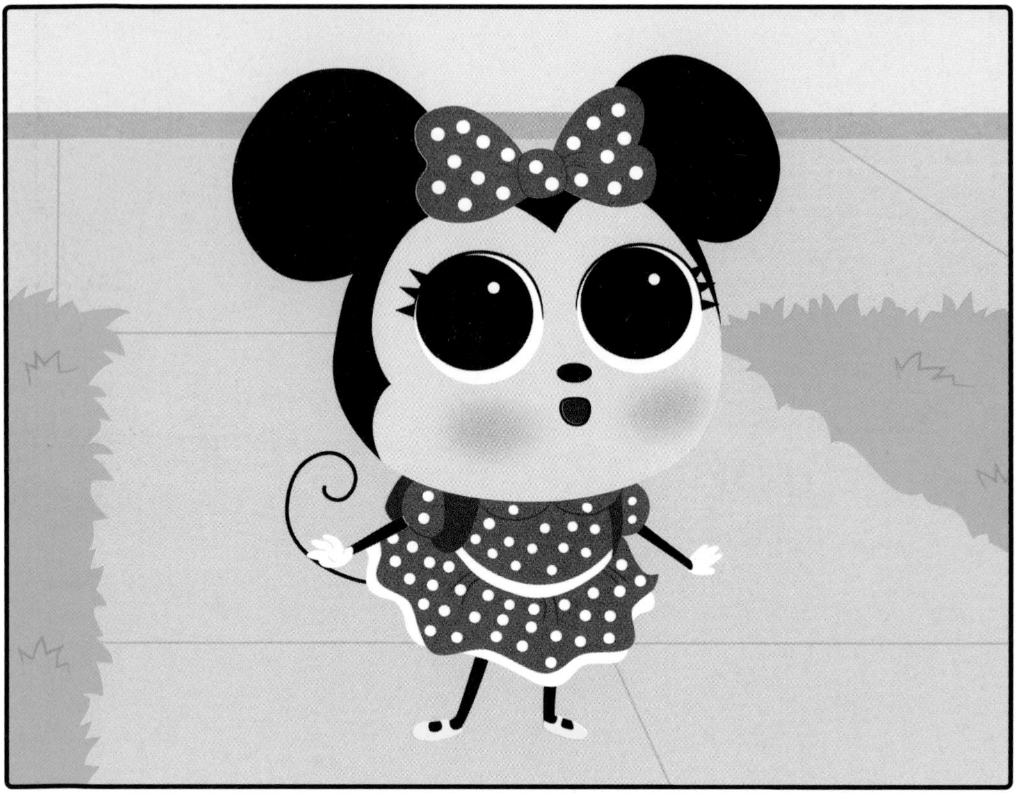

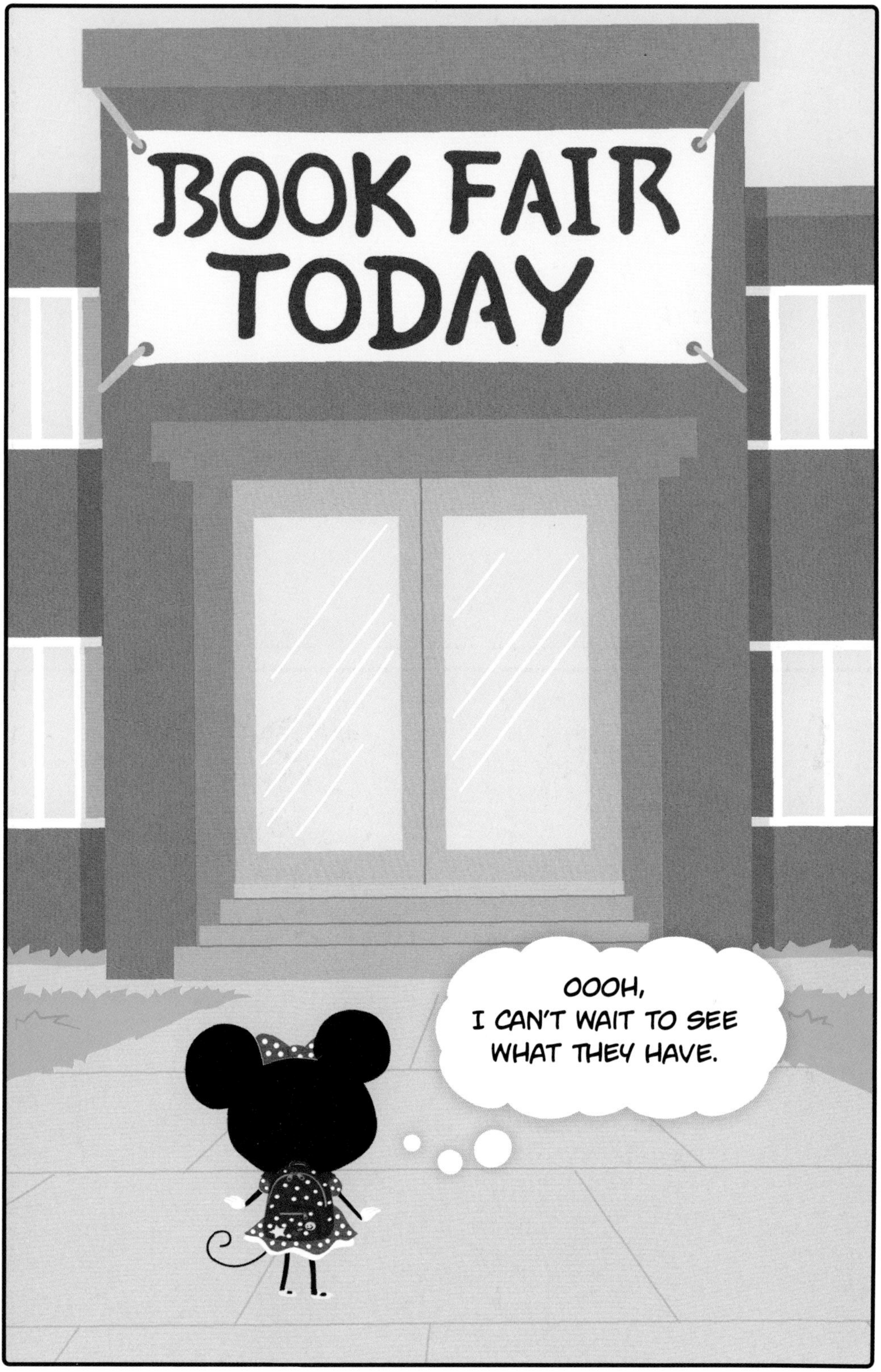
BOOK FAIR TODAY
OOOH, I CAN'T WAIT TO SEE WHAT THEY HAVE.

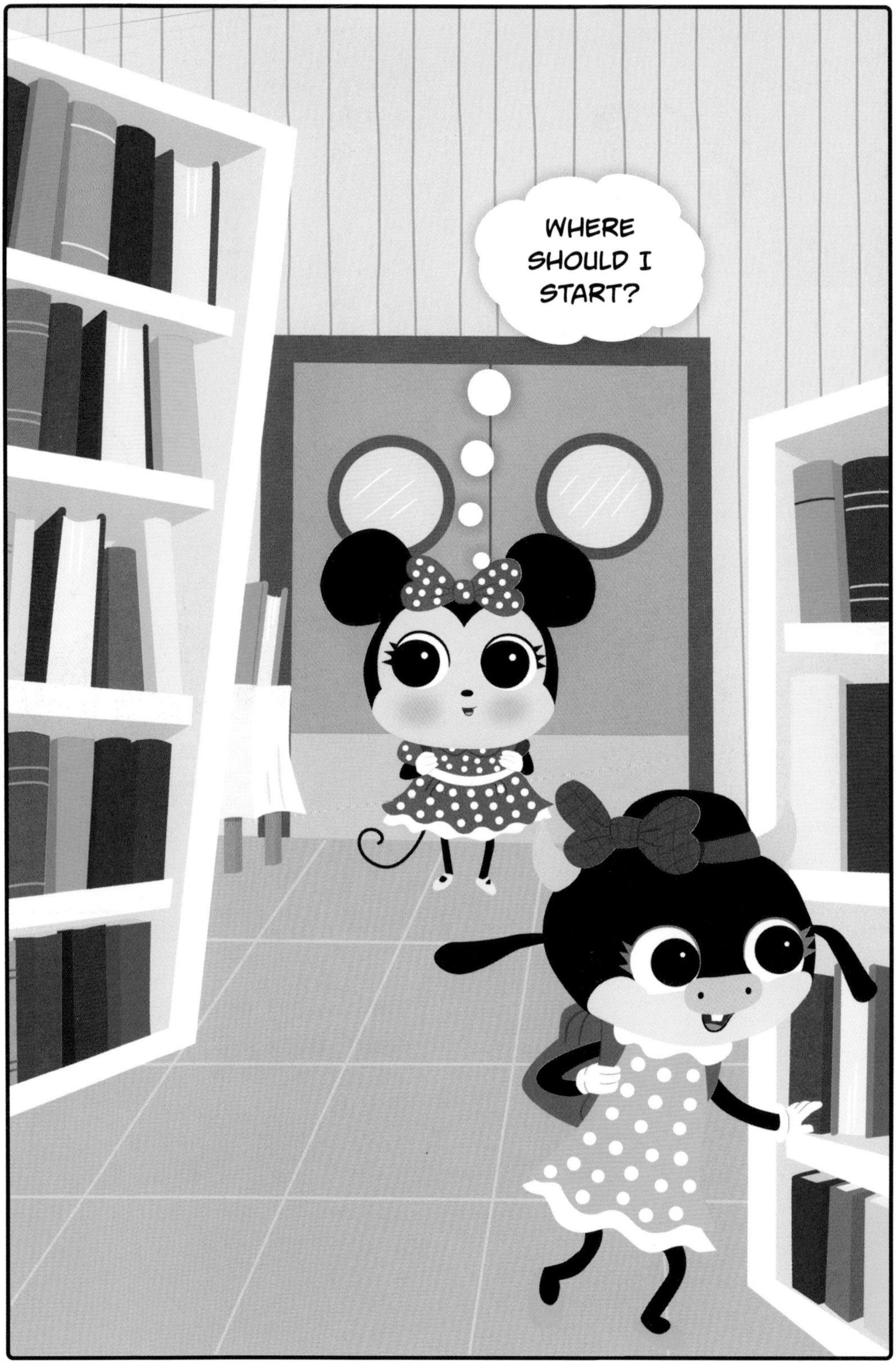
WHERE SHOULD I START?

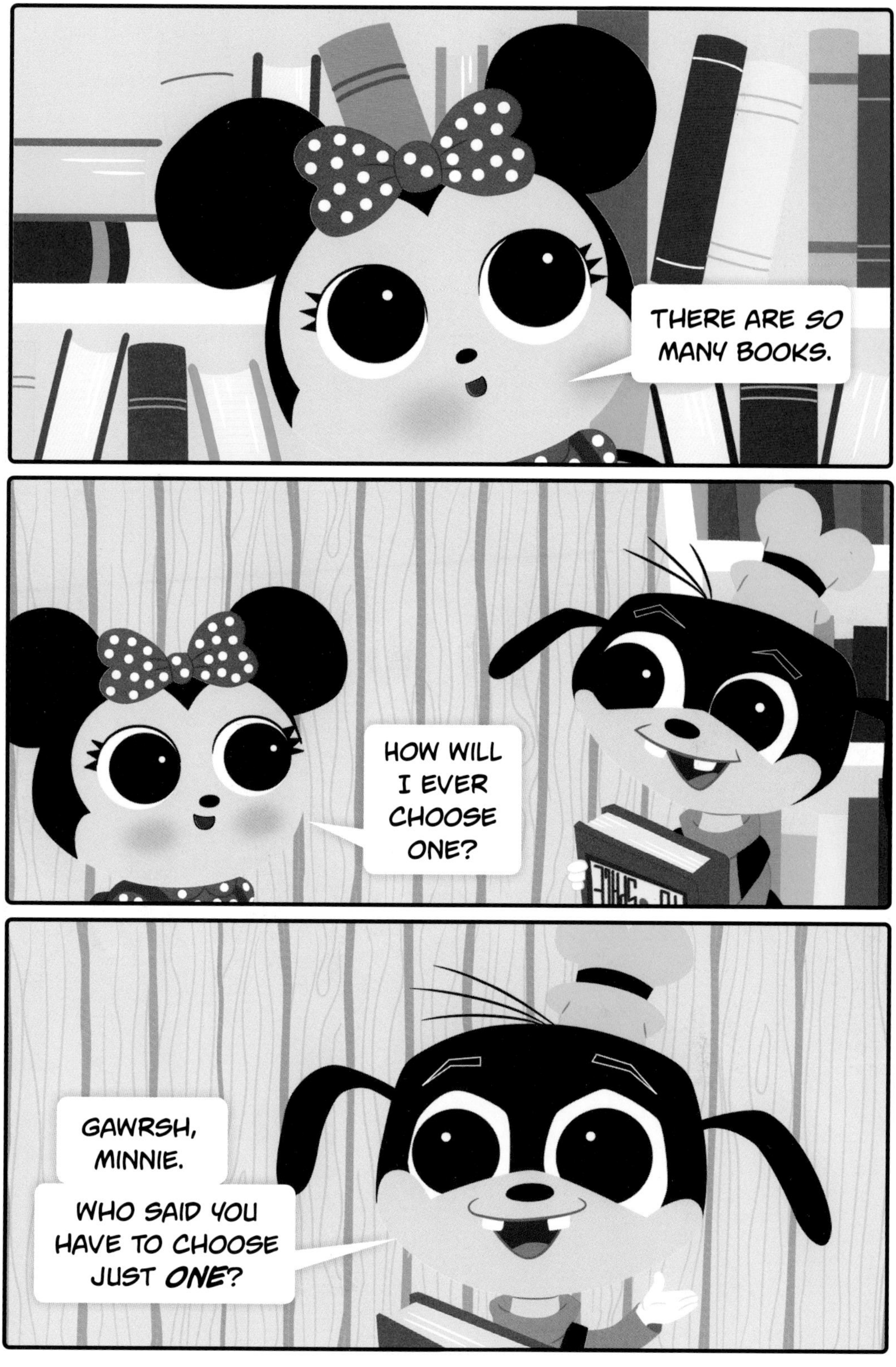
THERE ARE SO MANY BOOKS.
HOW WILL I EVER CHOOSE ONE?
GAWRSH, MINNIE.
WHO SAID YOU HAVE TO CHOOSE JUST *ONE*?

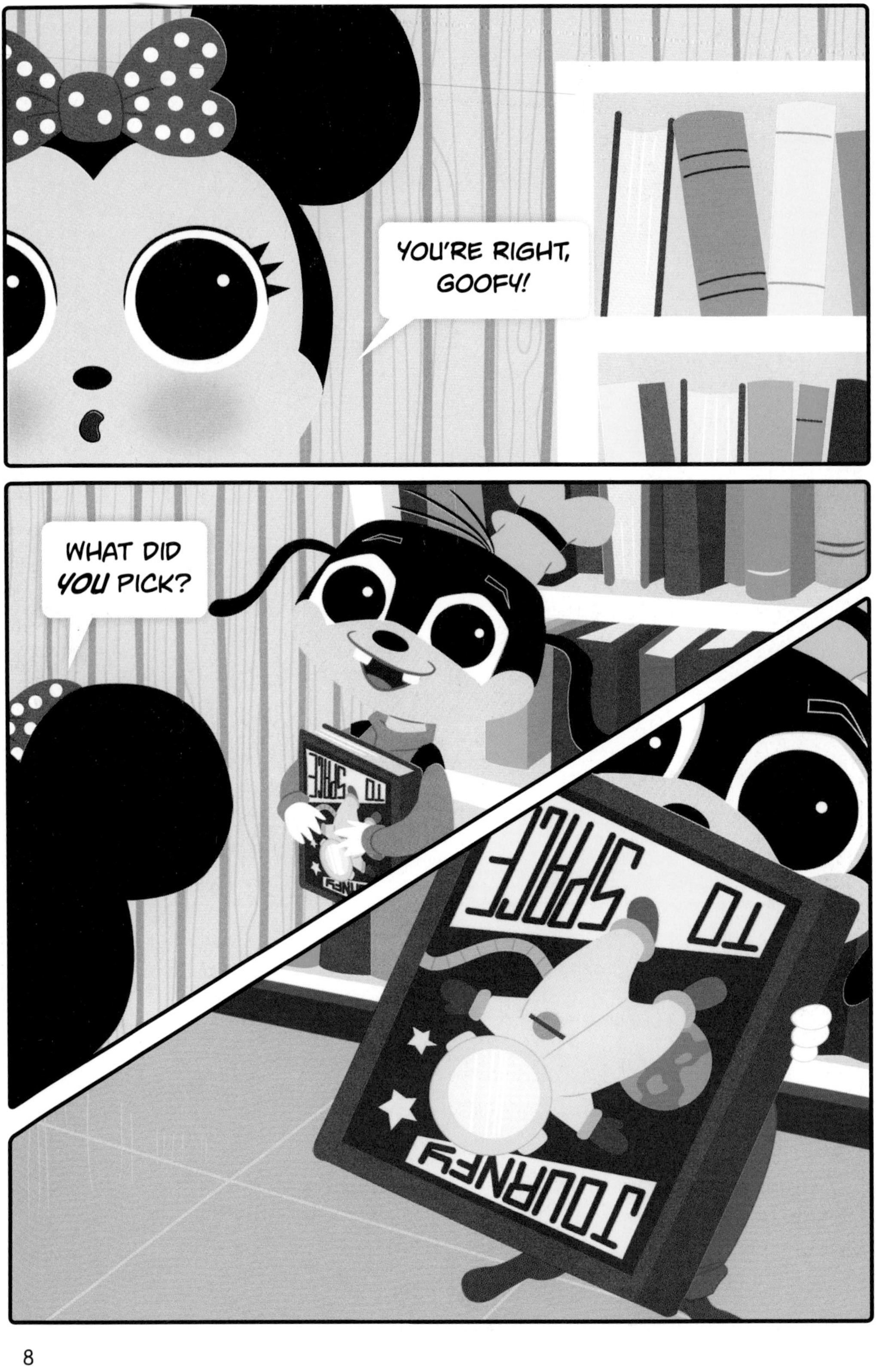
YOU'RE RIGHT, GOOFY!
WHAT DID *YOU* PICK?

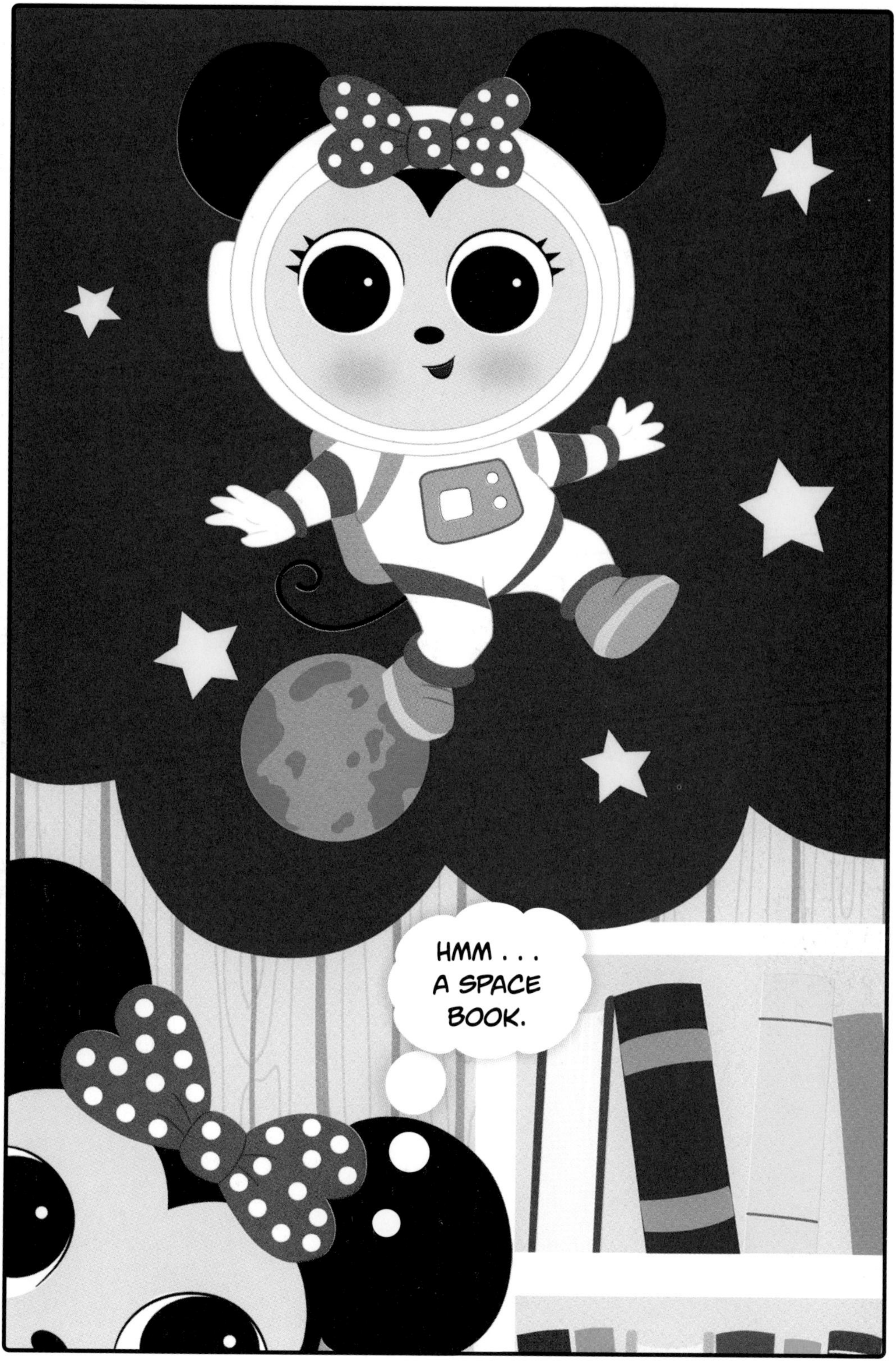
HMM . . . A SPACE BOOK.

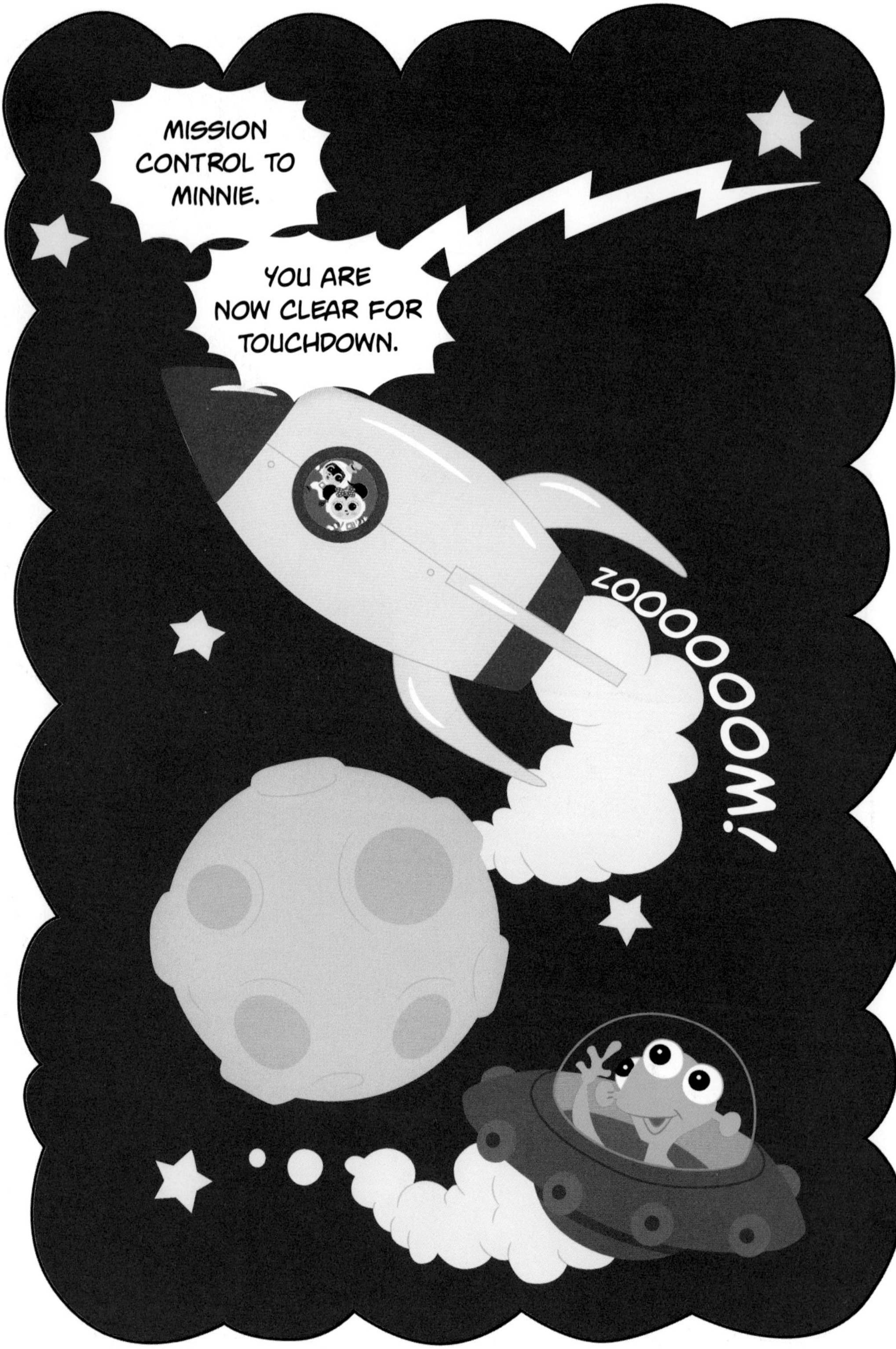
MISSION CONTROL TO MINNIE.
YOU ARE NOW CLEAR FOR TOUCHDOWN.
ZOOOOOOOM!

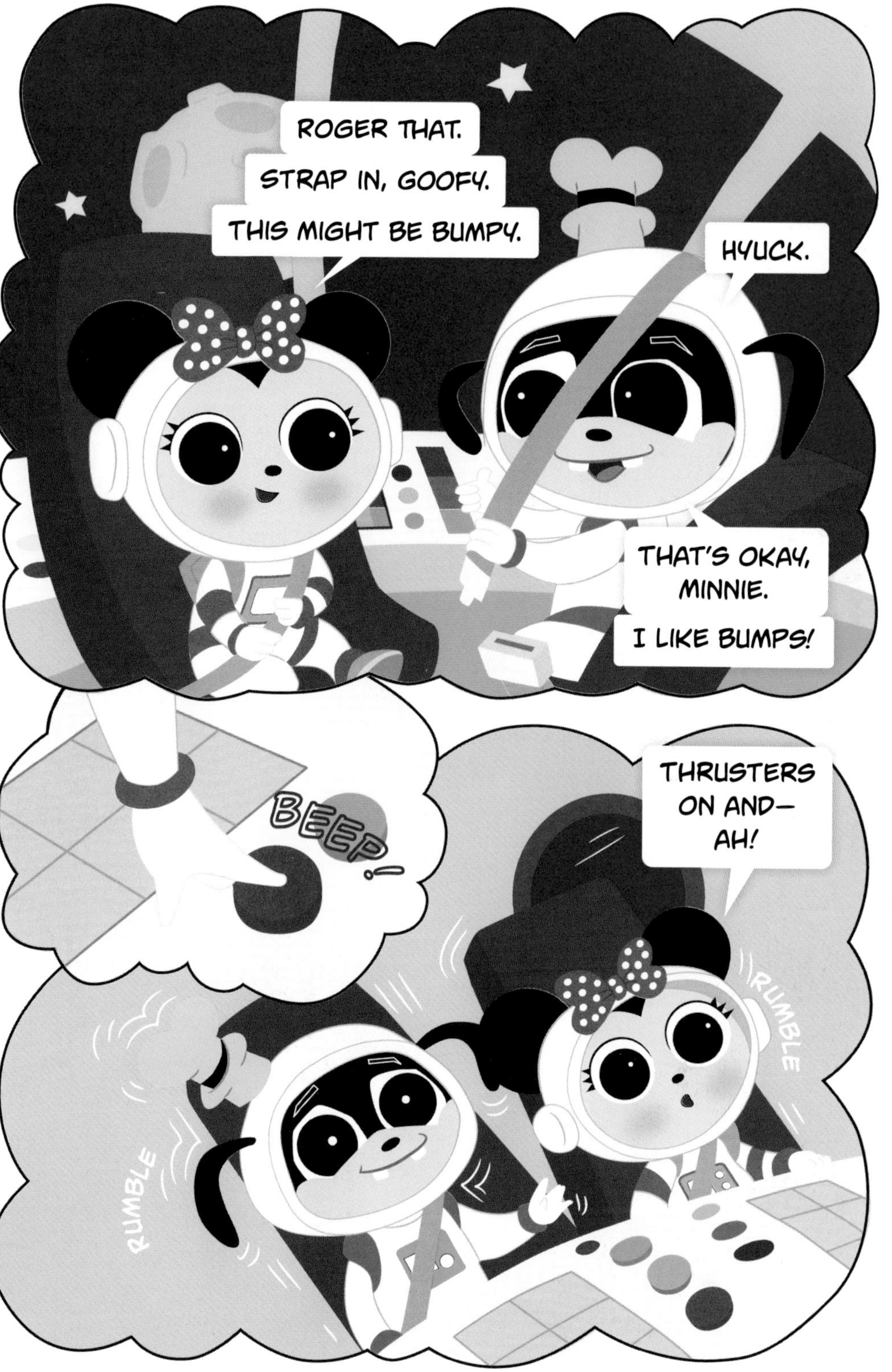
ROGER THAT.
STRAP IN, GOOFY.
THIS MIGHT BE BUMPY.
HYUCK.
THAT'S OKAY, MINNIE.
I LIKE BUMPS!
BEEP!
THRUSTERS ON AND—
AH!
RUMBLE
RUMBLE

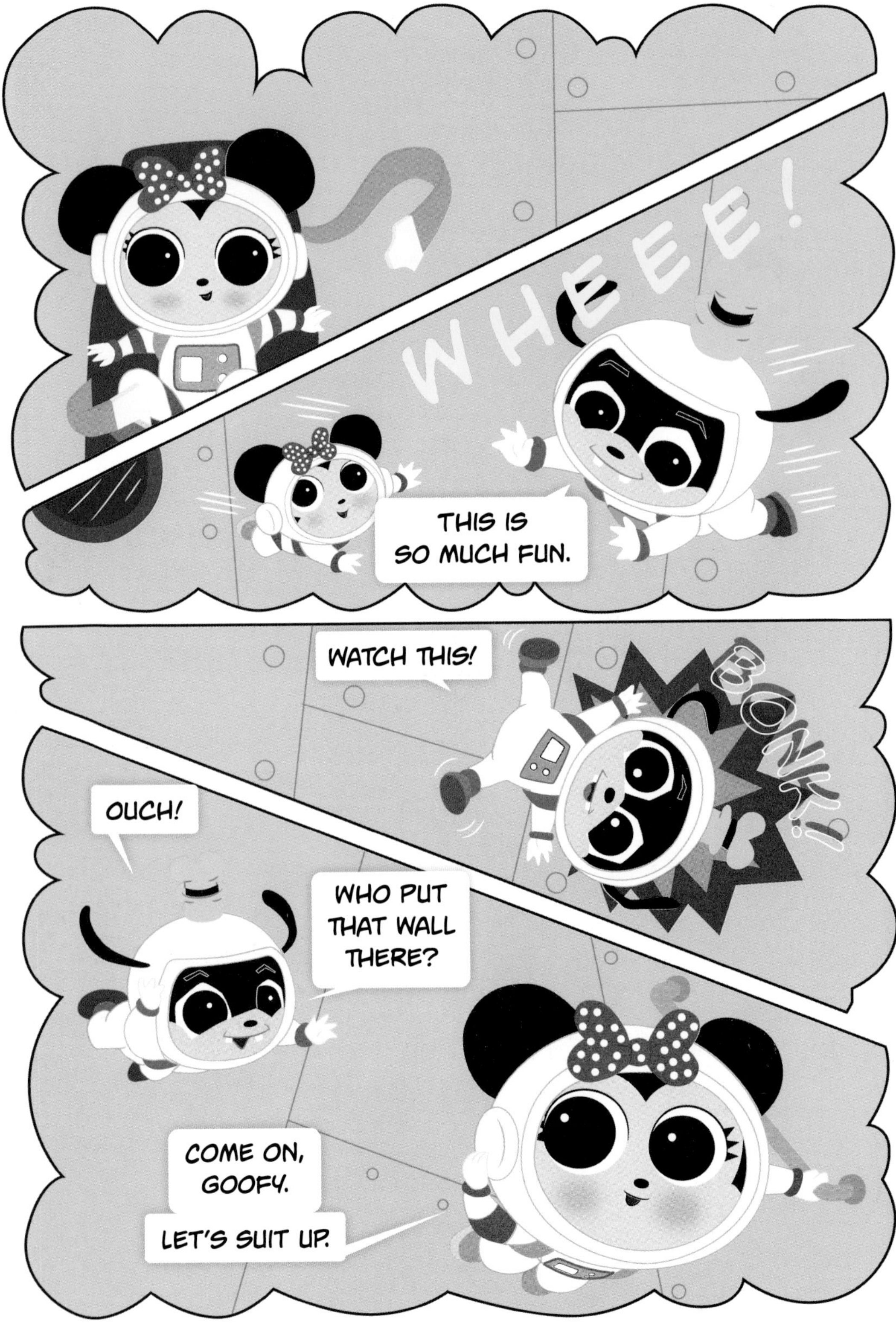
WHEEEE!
THIS IS SO MUCH FUN.
WATCH THIS!
BONK!
OUCH!
WHO PUT THAT WALL THERE?
COME ON, GOOFY.
LET'S SUIT UP.

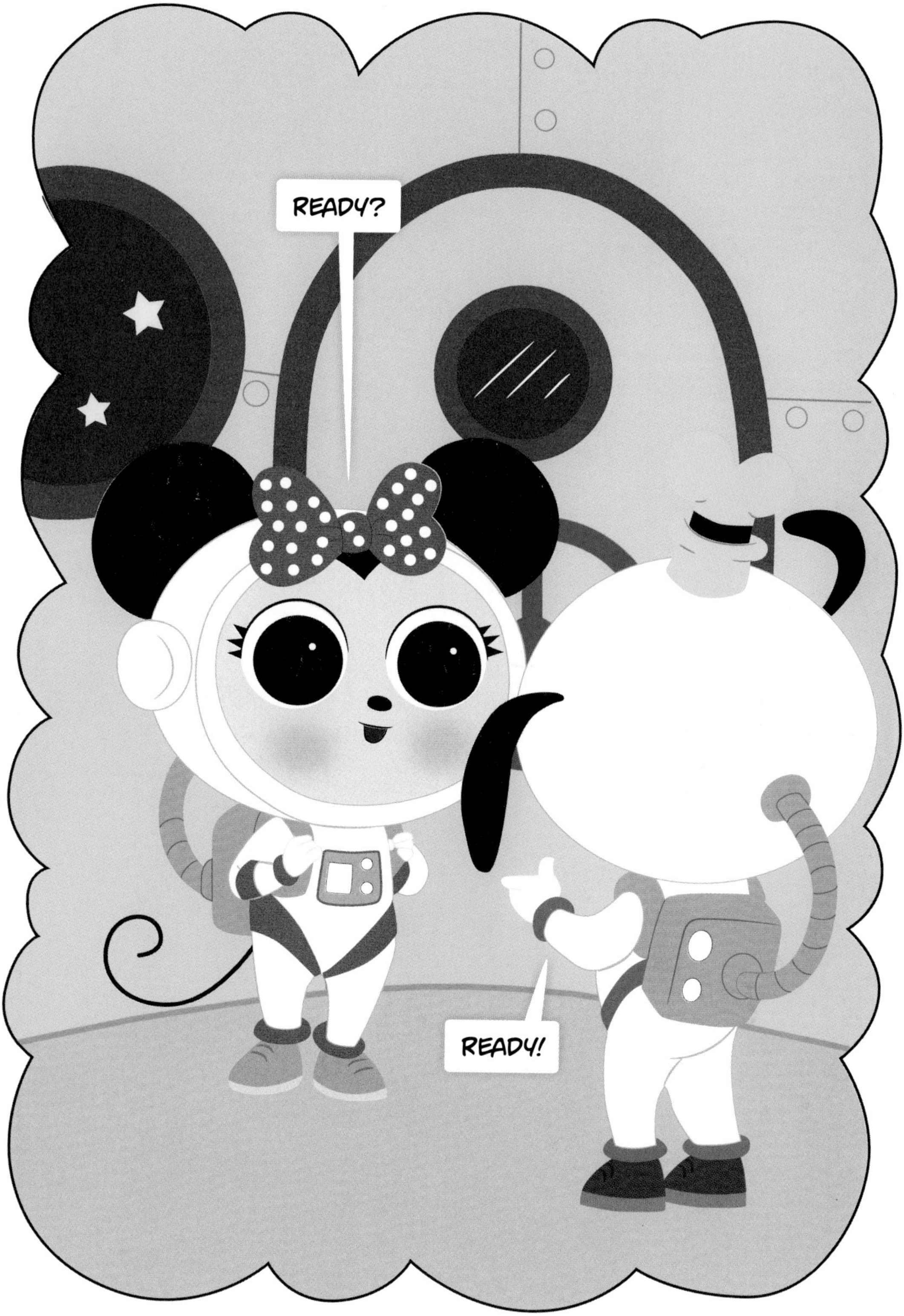
READY?
READY!

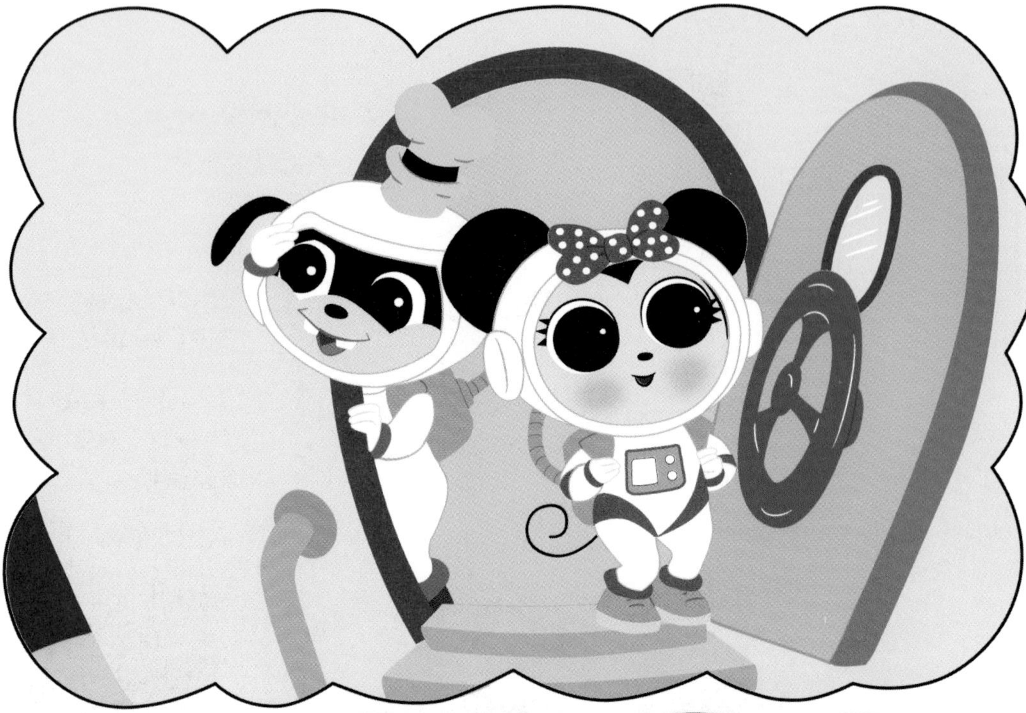

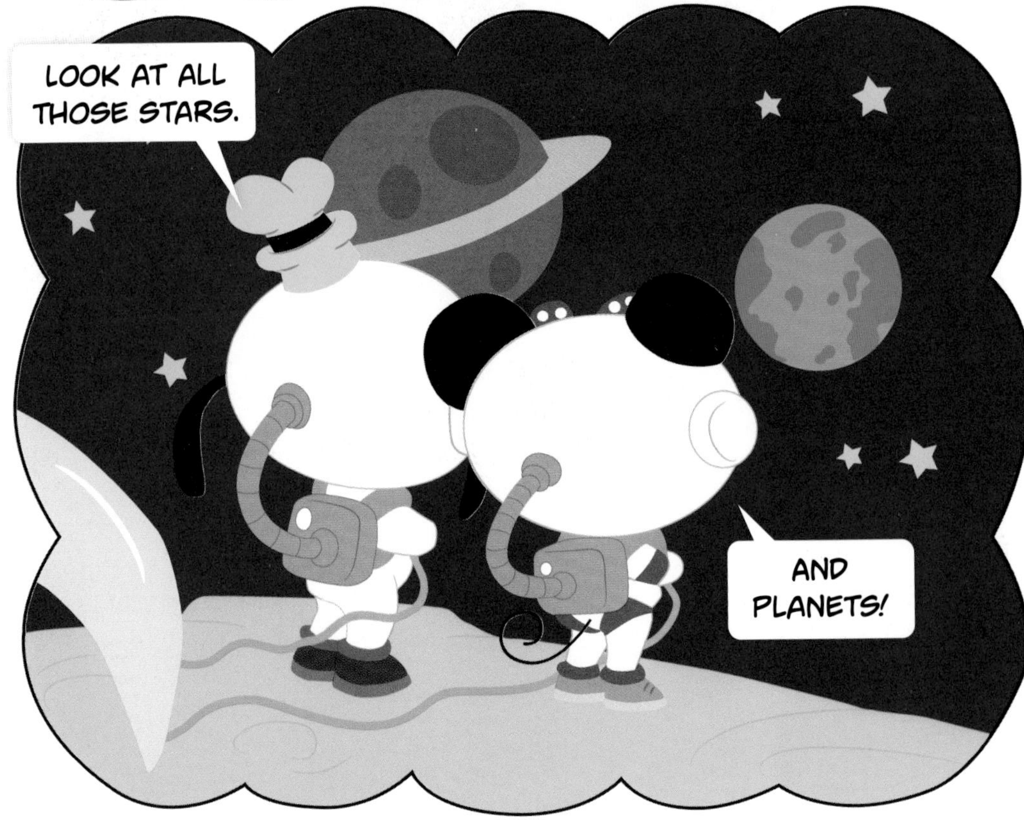
LOOK AT ALL THOSE STARS.
AND PLANETS!

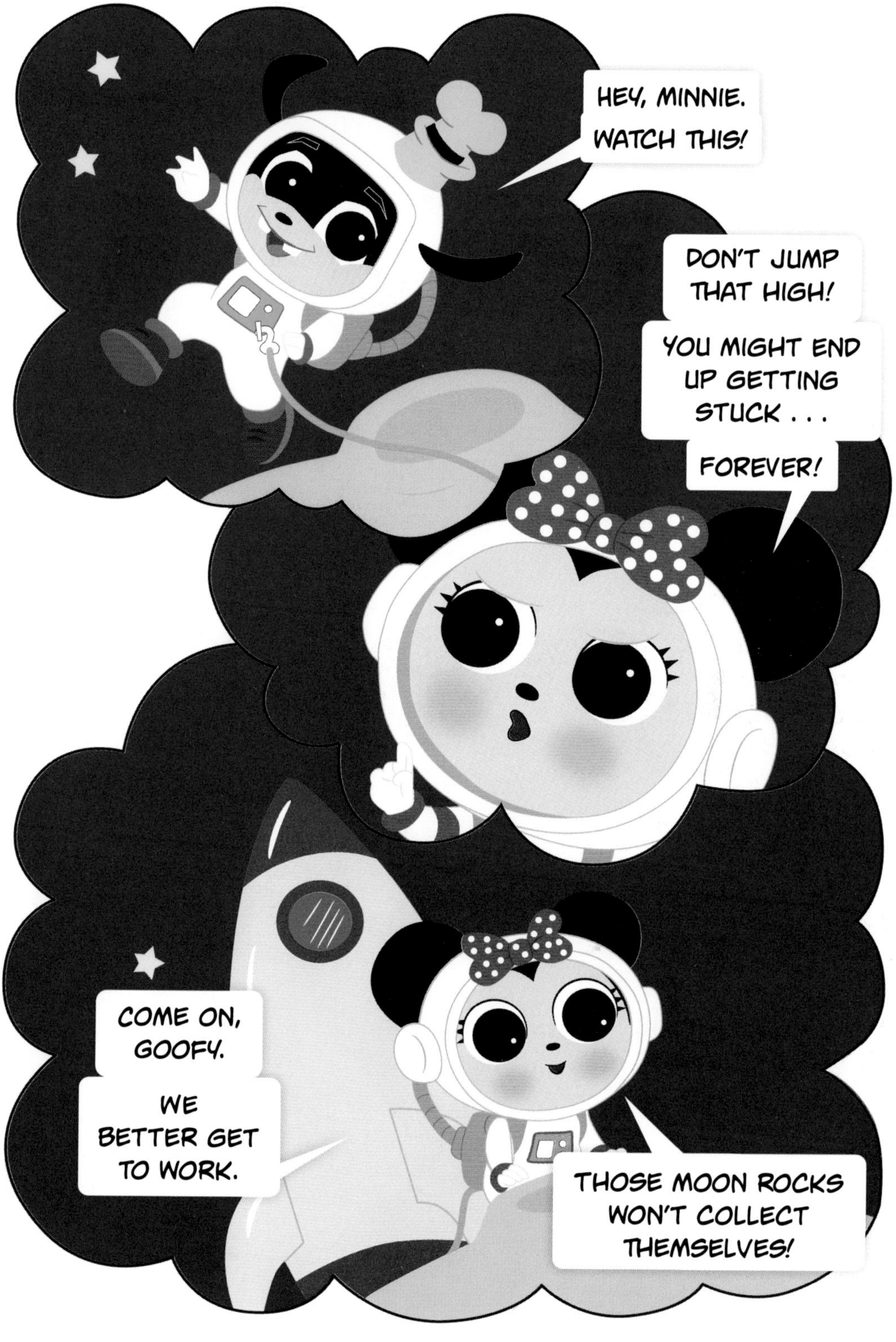
HEY, MINNIE.
WATCH THIS!
DON'T JUMP THAT HIGH!
YOU MIGHT END UP GETTING STUCK . . .
FOREVER!
COME ON, GOOFY.
WE BETTER GET TO WORK.
THOSE MOON ROCKS WON'T COLLECT THEMSELVES!

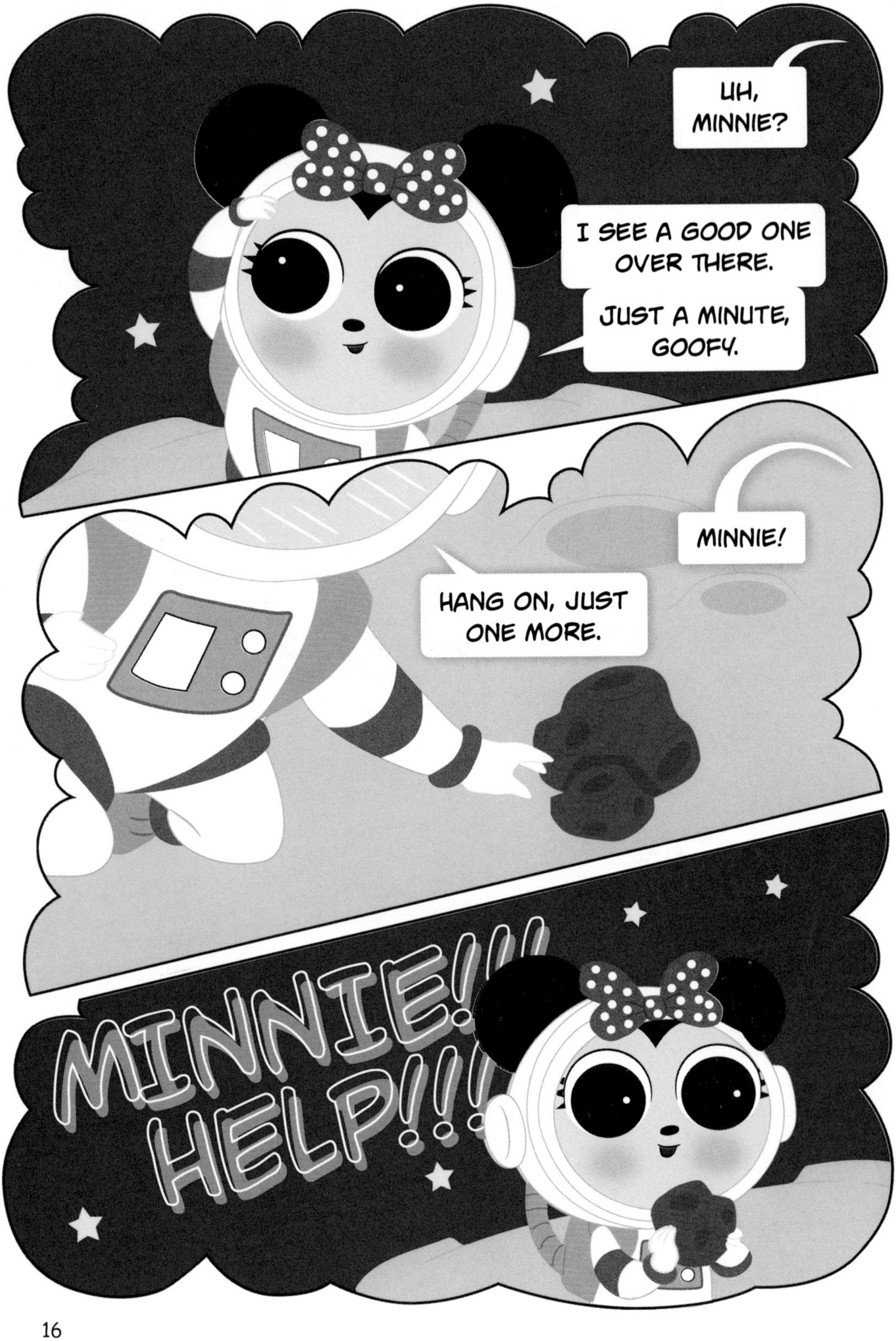
UH, MINNIE?
I SEE A GOOD ONE OVER THERE.
JUST A MINUTE, GOOFY.
MINNIE!
HANG ON, JUST ONE MORE.
MINNIE!!! HELP!!!

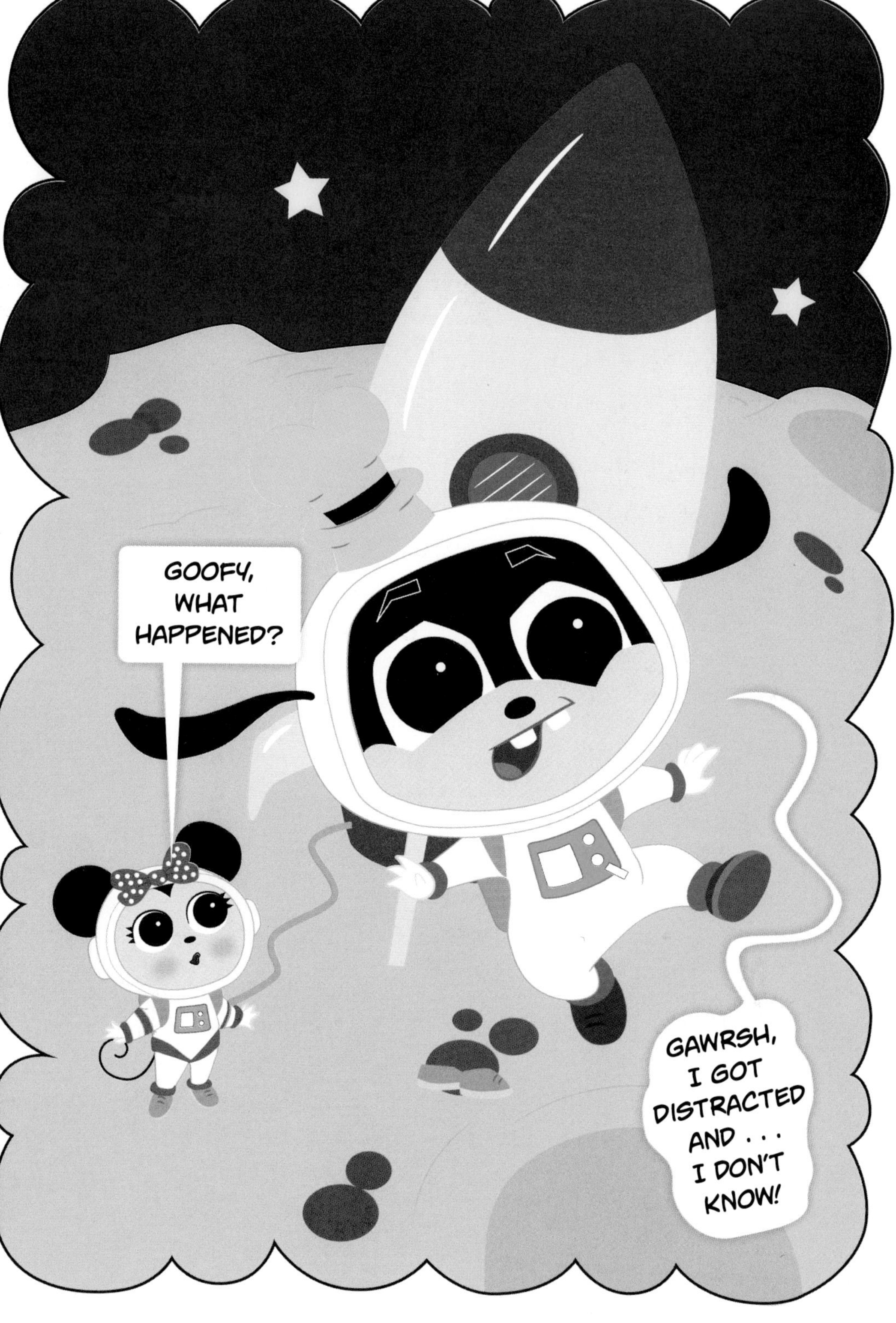
GOOFY, WHAT HAPPENED?
GAWRSH, I GOT DISTRACTED AND . . . I DON'T KNOW!

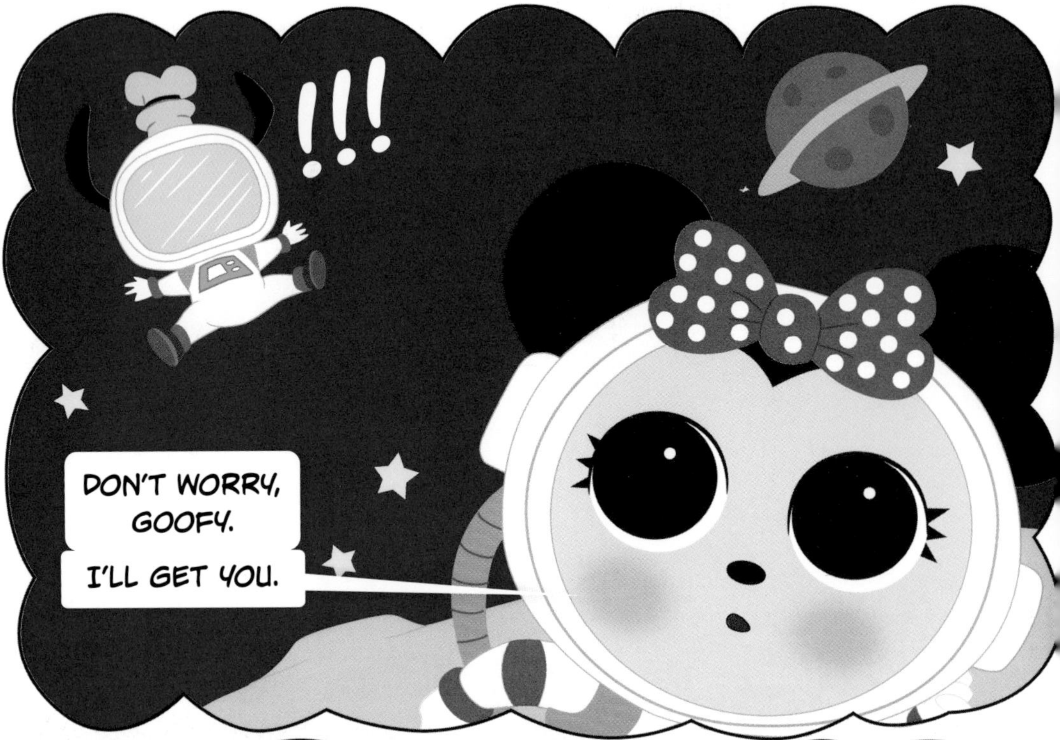
!!!
DON'T WORRY, GOOFY.
I'LL GET YOU.

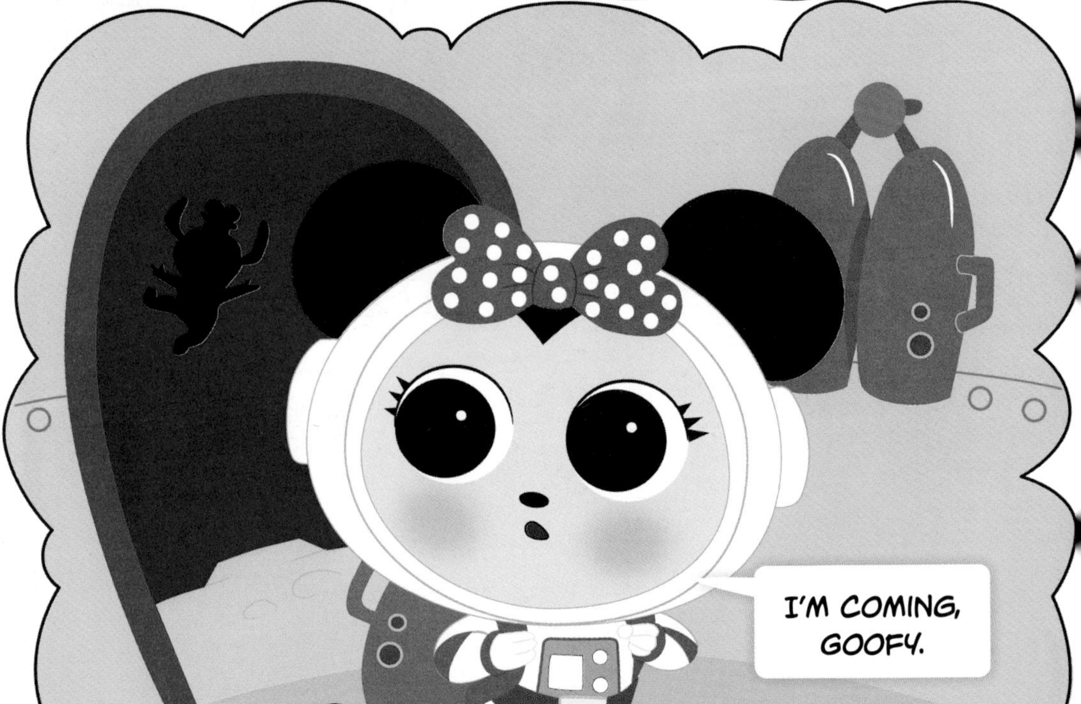
I'M COMING, GOOFY.

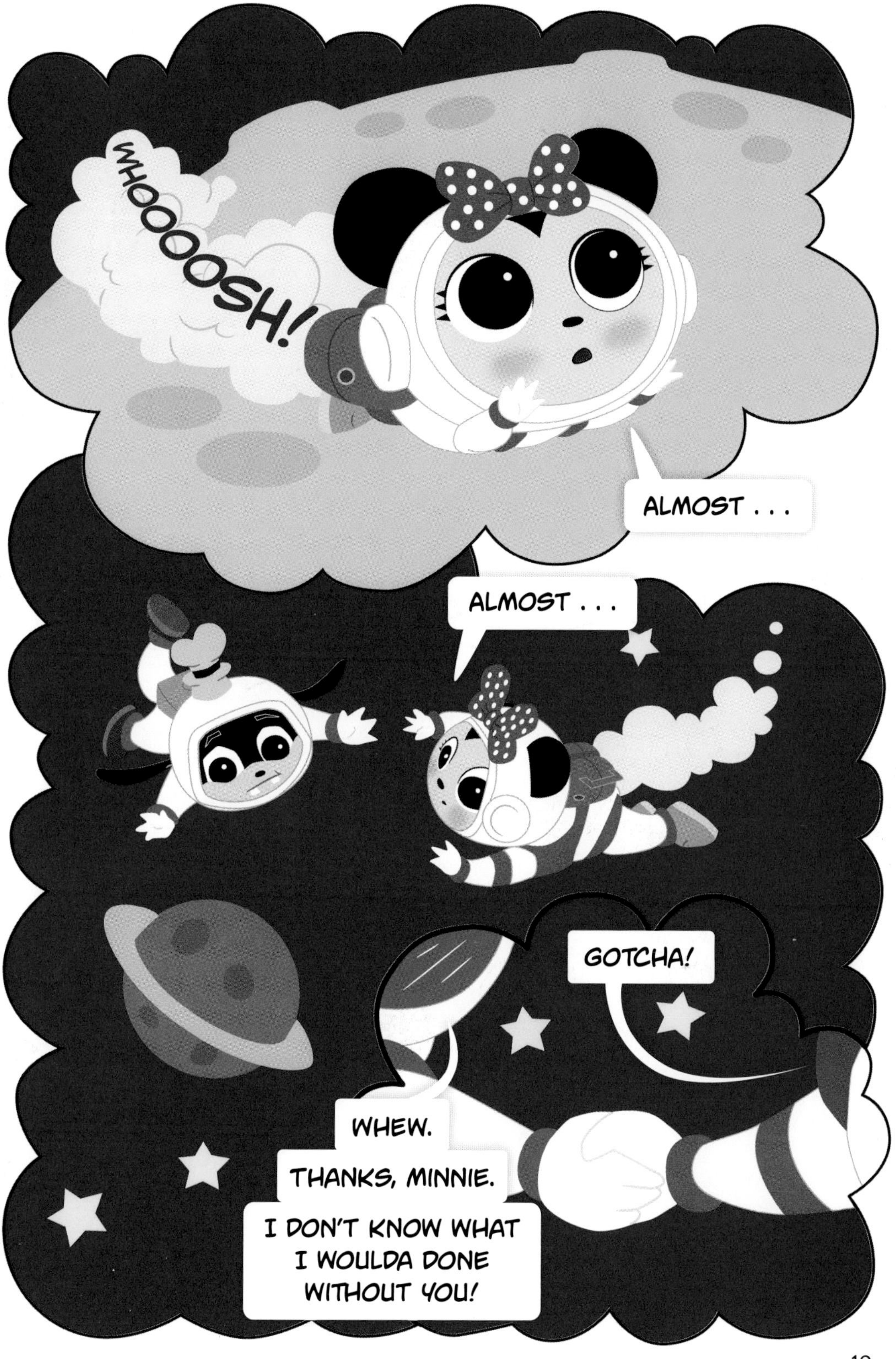
WHOOOOSH!
ALMOST . . .
ALMOST . . .
GOTCHA!
WHEW.
THANKS, MINNIE.
I DON'T KNOW WHAT I WOULDA DONE WITHOUT YOU!

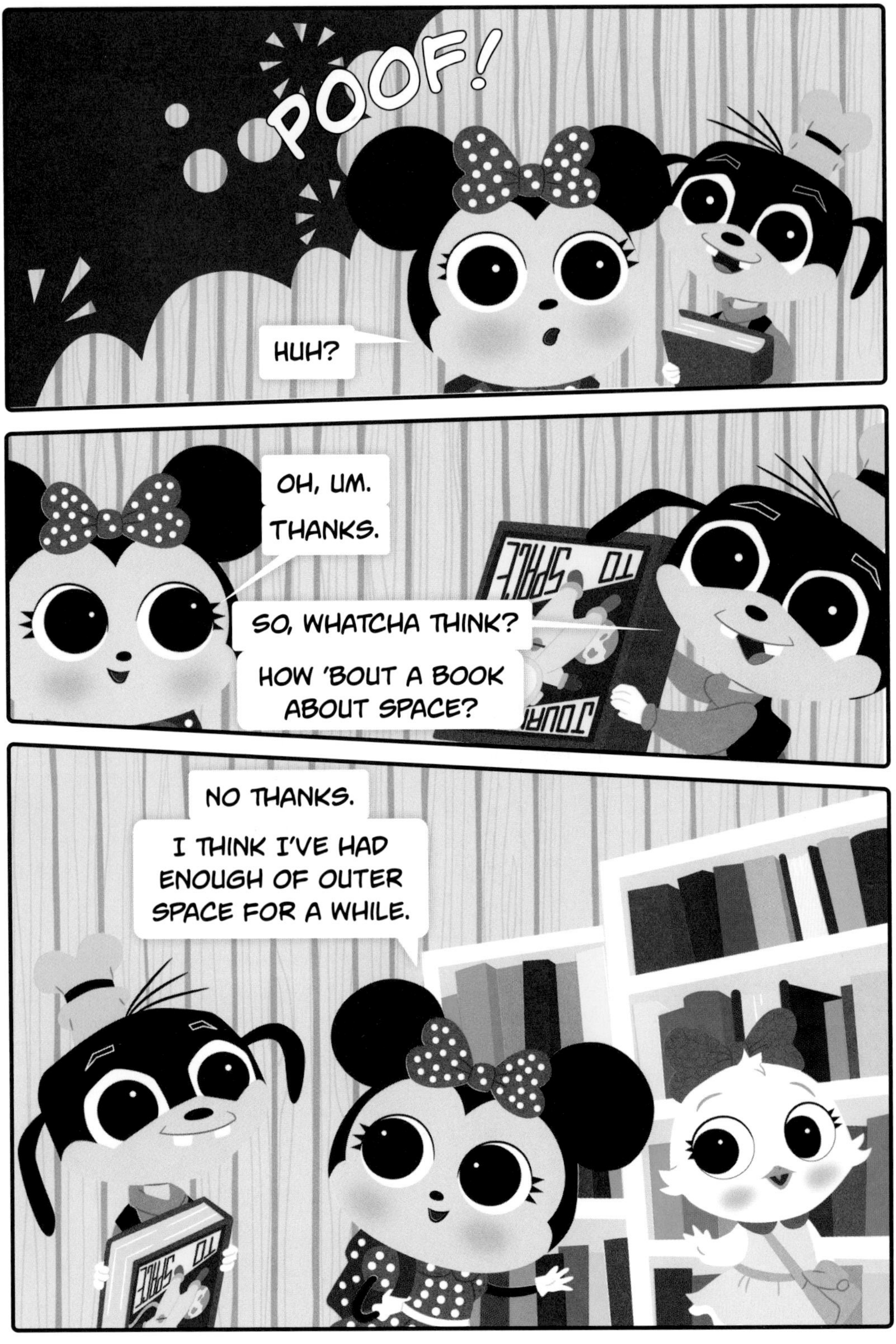
POOF!
HUH?
OH, UM.
THANKS.
SO, WHATCHA THINK?
HOW 'BOUT A BOOK ABOUT SPACE?
NO THANKS.
I THINK I'VE HAD ENOUGH OF OUTER SPACE FOR A WHILE.

PART 2

CHEF MINNIE

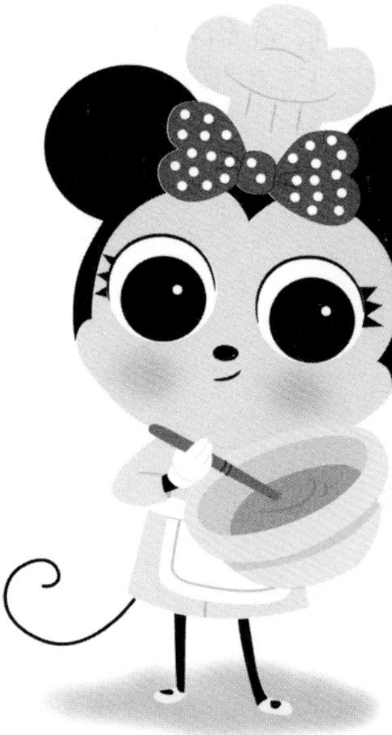

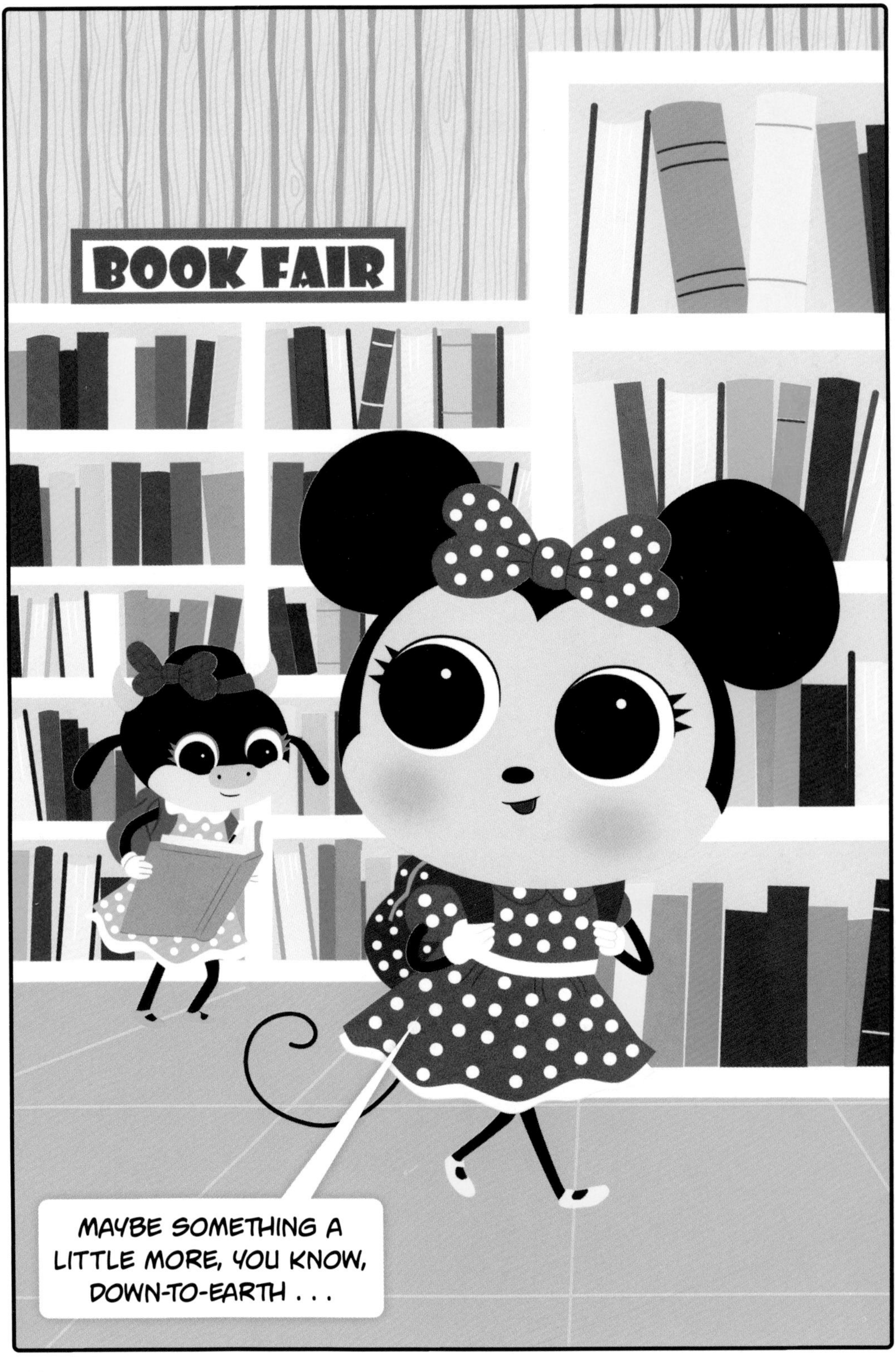
BOOK FAIR
MAYBE SOMETHING A LITTLE MORE, YOU KNOW, DOWN-TO-EARTH . . .

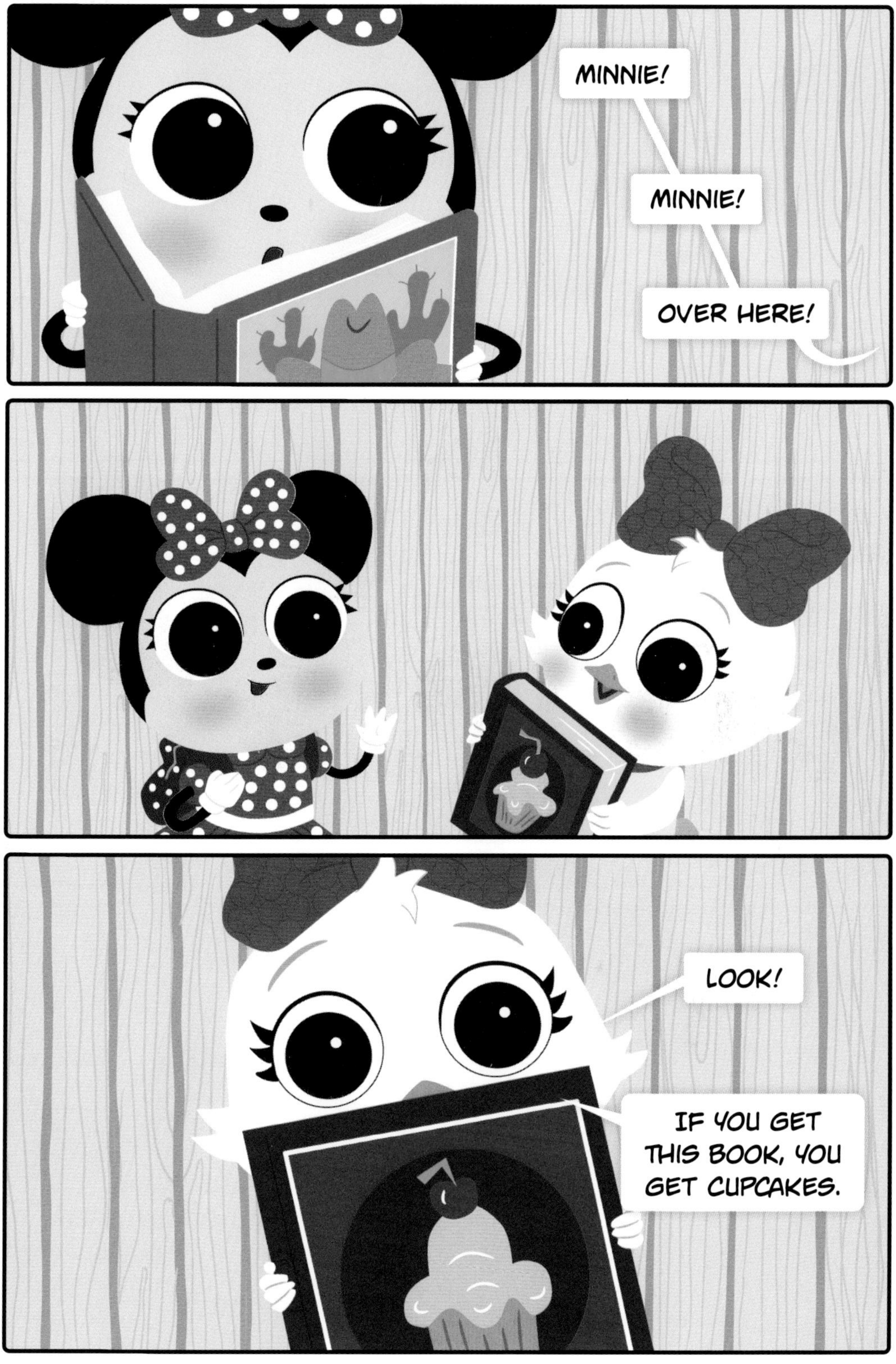
MINNIE!
MINNIE!
OVER HERE!
LOOK!
IF YOU GET THIS BOOK, YOU GET CUPCAKES.

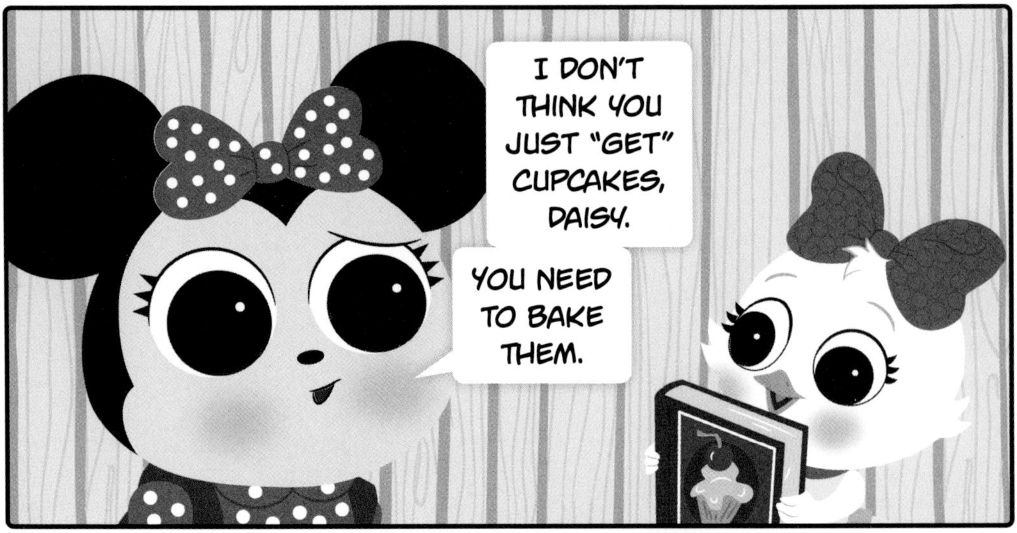
I DON'T THINK YOU JUST "GET" CUPCAKES, DAISY.
YOU NEED TO BAKE THEM.
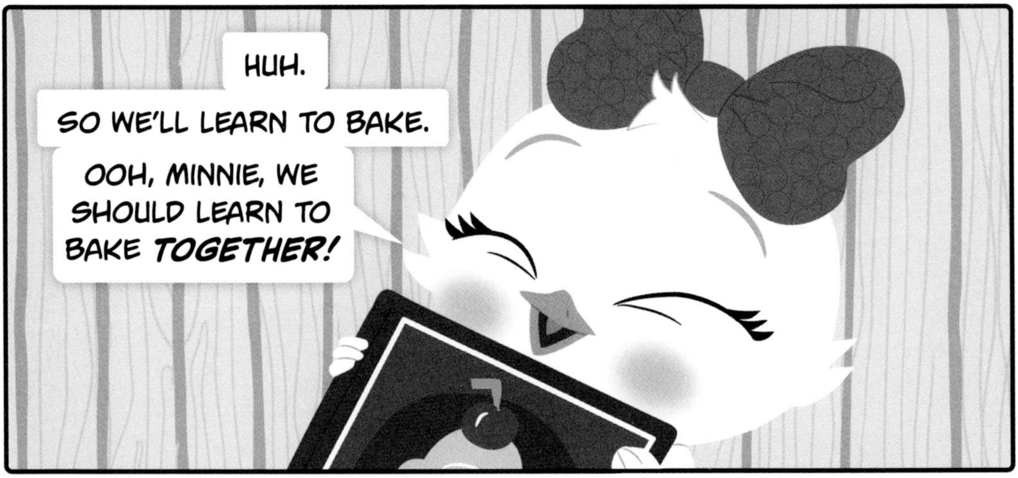
HUH.
SO WE'LL LEARN TO BAKE.
OOH, MINNIE, WE SHOULD LEARN TO BAKE *TOGETHER!*
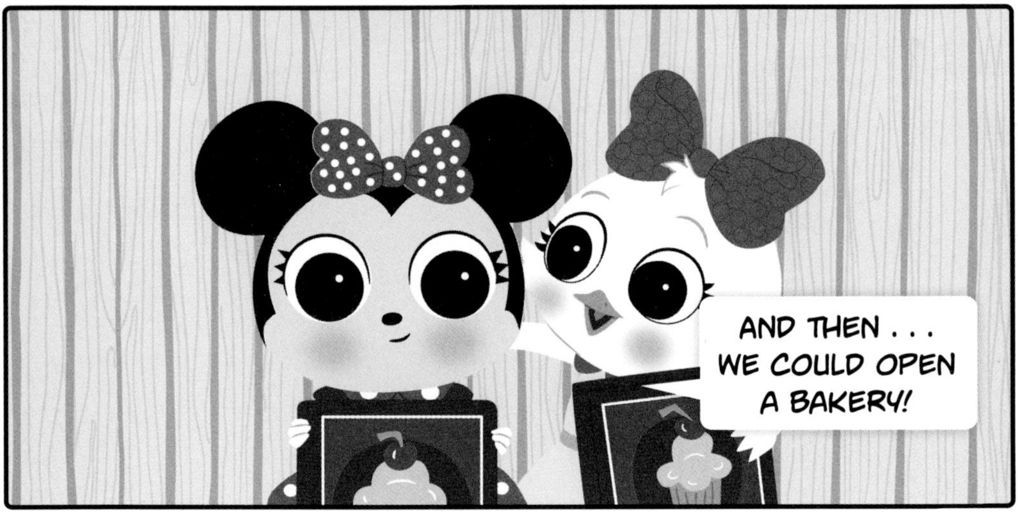
AND THEN . . . WE COULD OPEN A BAKERY!

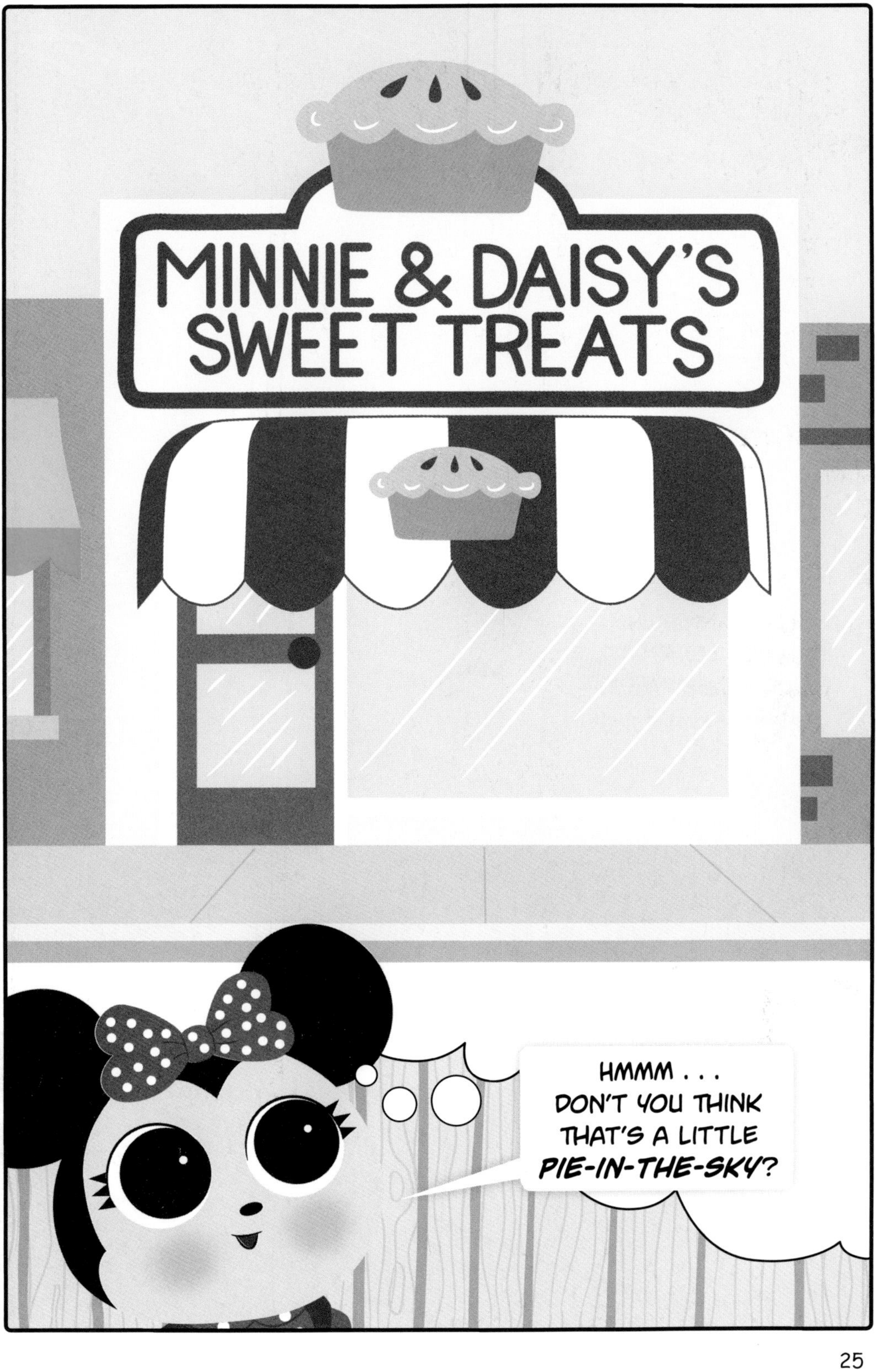
MINNIE & DAISY'S SWEET TREATS
HMMM . . . DON'T YOU THINK THAT'S A LITTLE *PIE-IN-THE-SKY*?

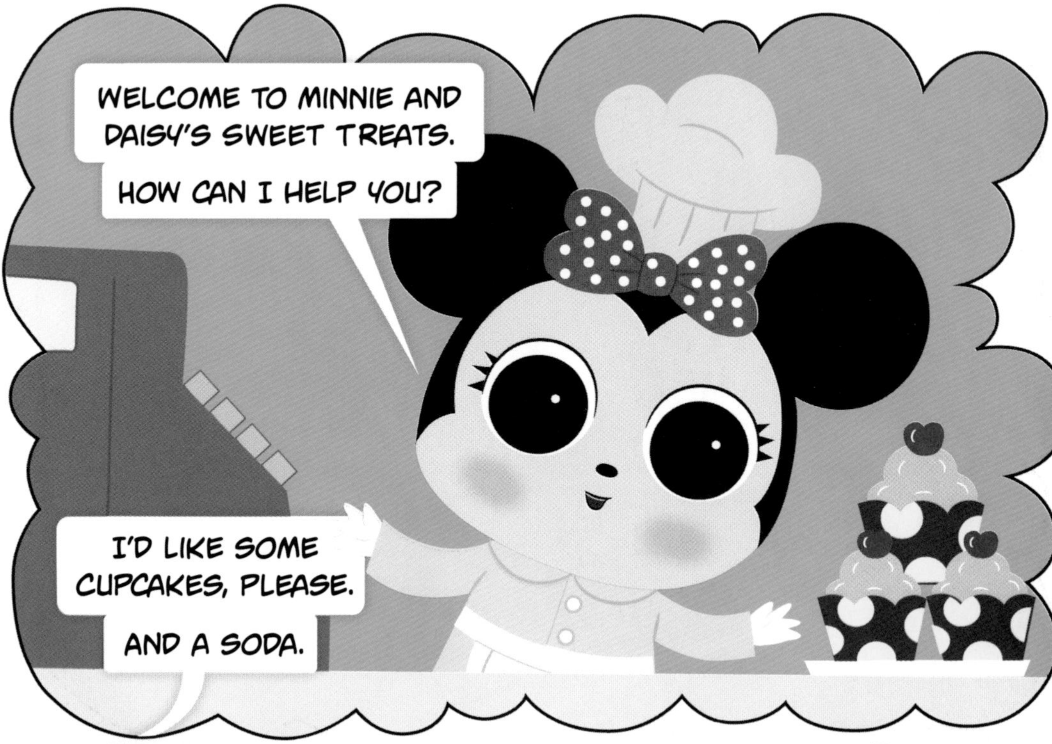
WELCOME TO MINNIE AND DAISY'S SWEET TREATS.
HOW CAN I HELP YOU?
I'D LIKE SOME CUPCAKES, PLEASE.
AND A SODA.

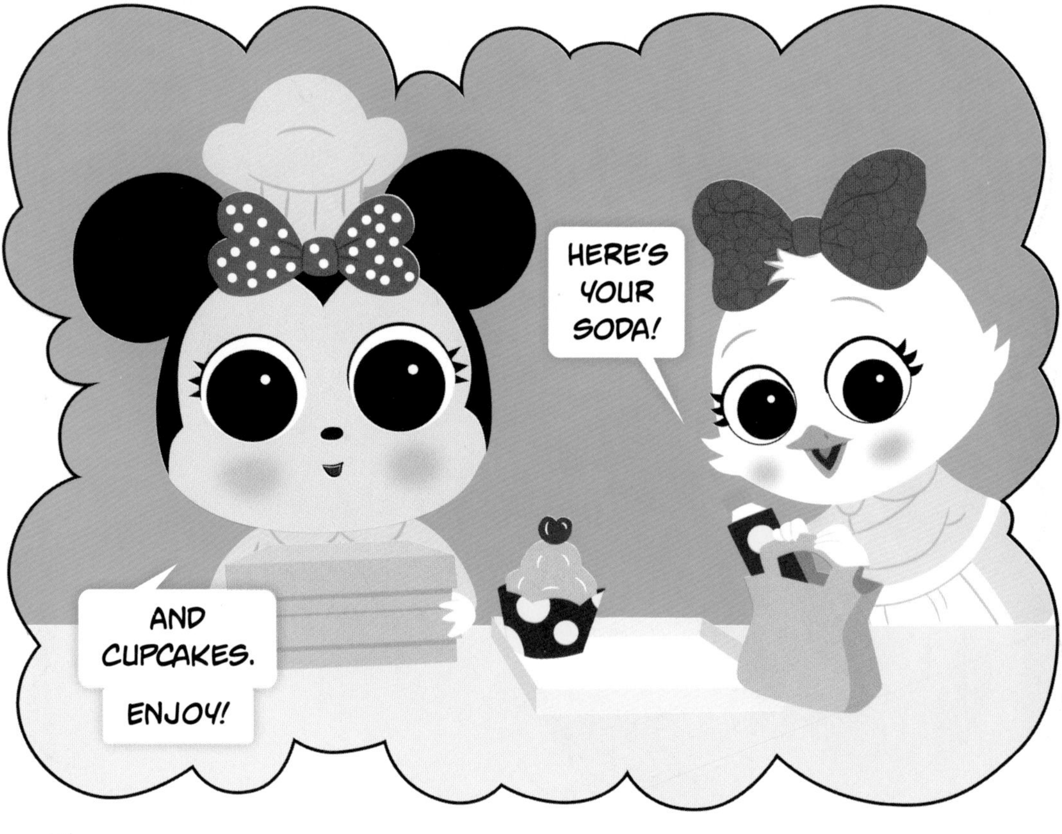
HERE'S YOUR SODA!
AND CUPCAKES.
ENJOY!

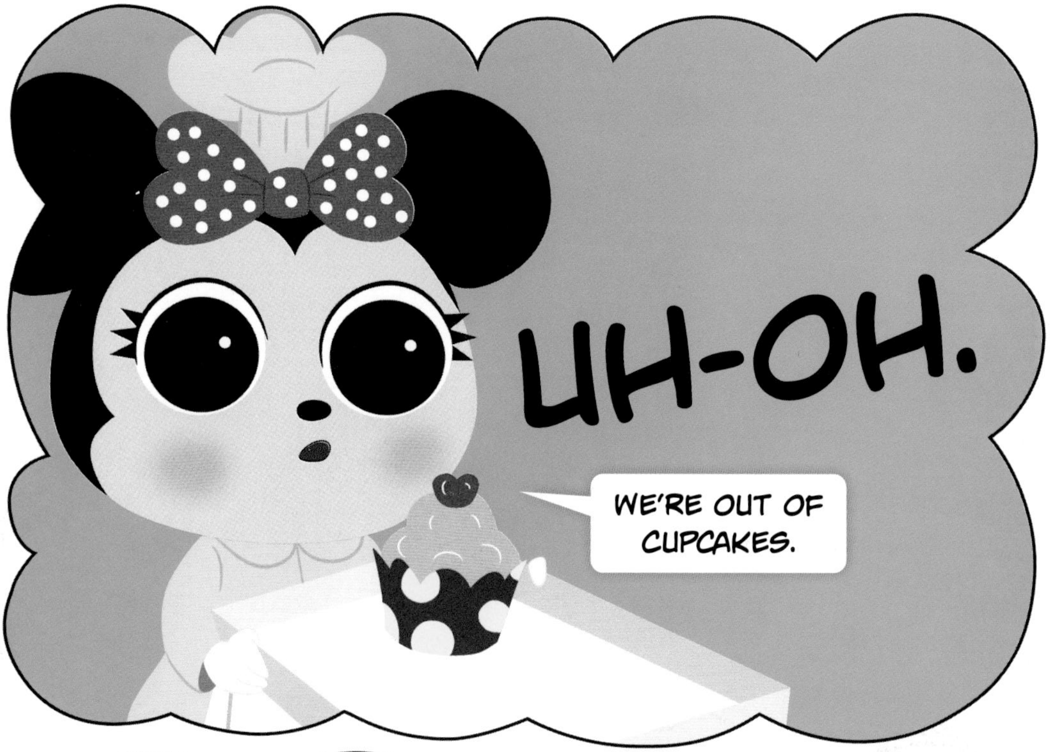
UH-OH.
WE'RE OUT OF CUPCAKES.

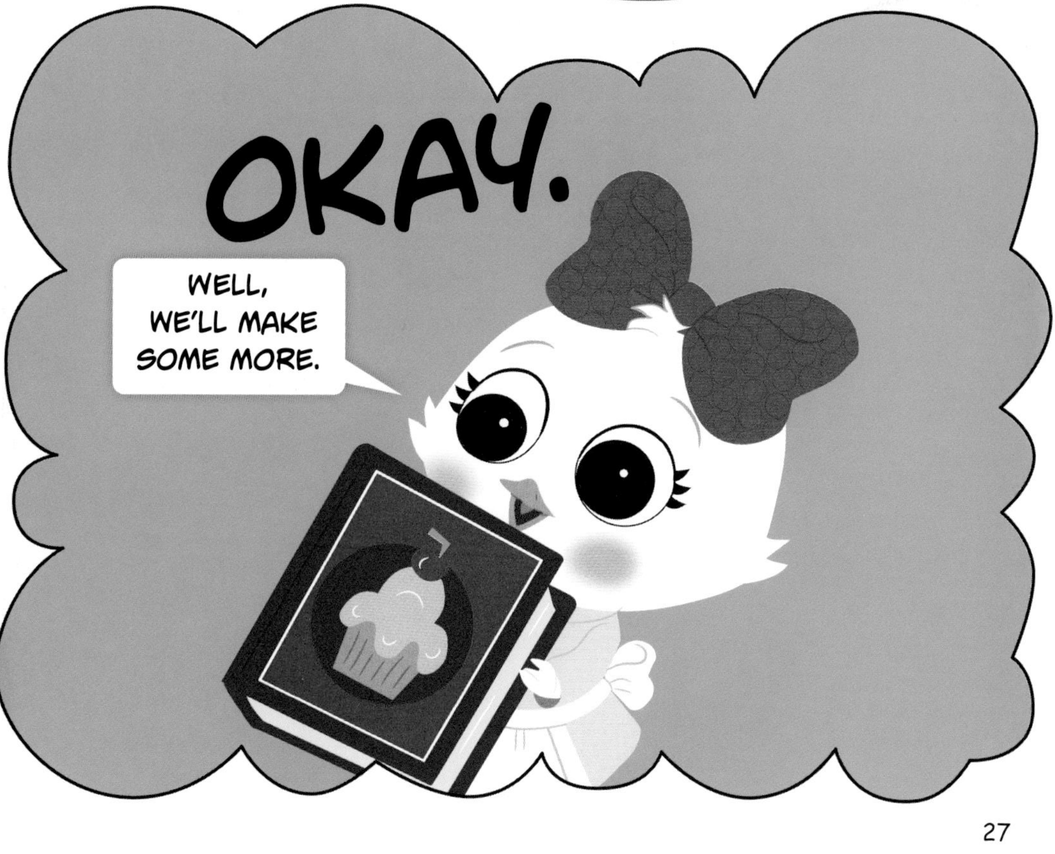
OKAY.
WELL, WE'LL MAKE SOME MORE.

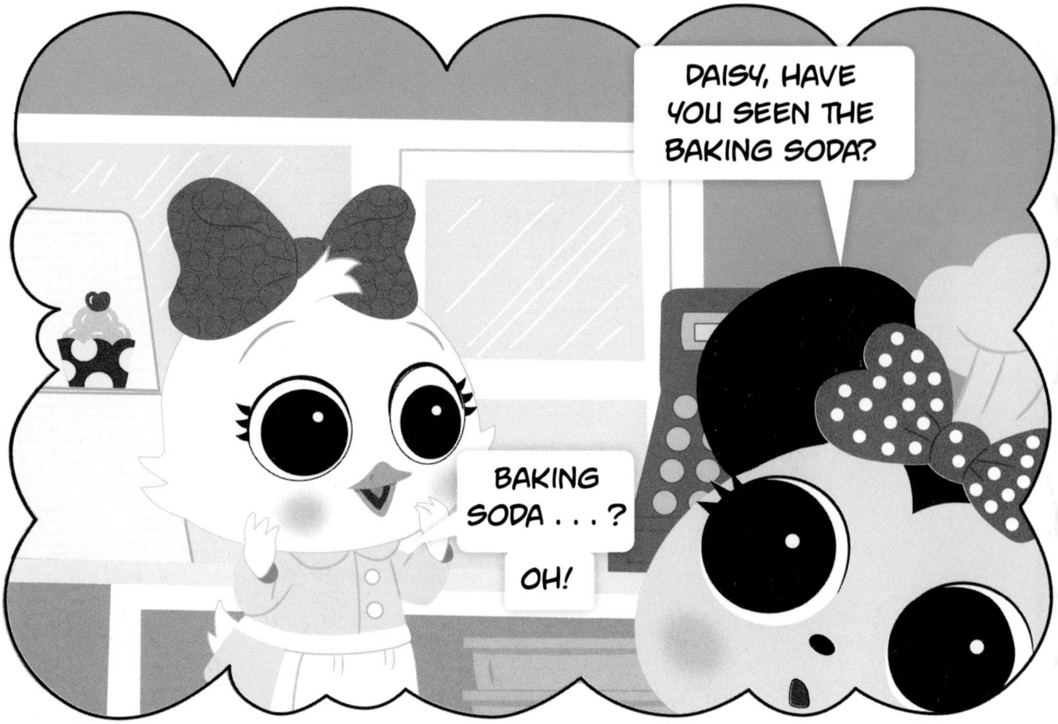
DAISY, HAVE YOU SEEN THE BAKING SODA?
BAKING SODA . . . ?
OH!

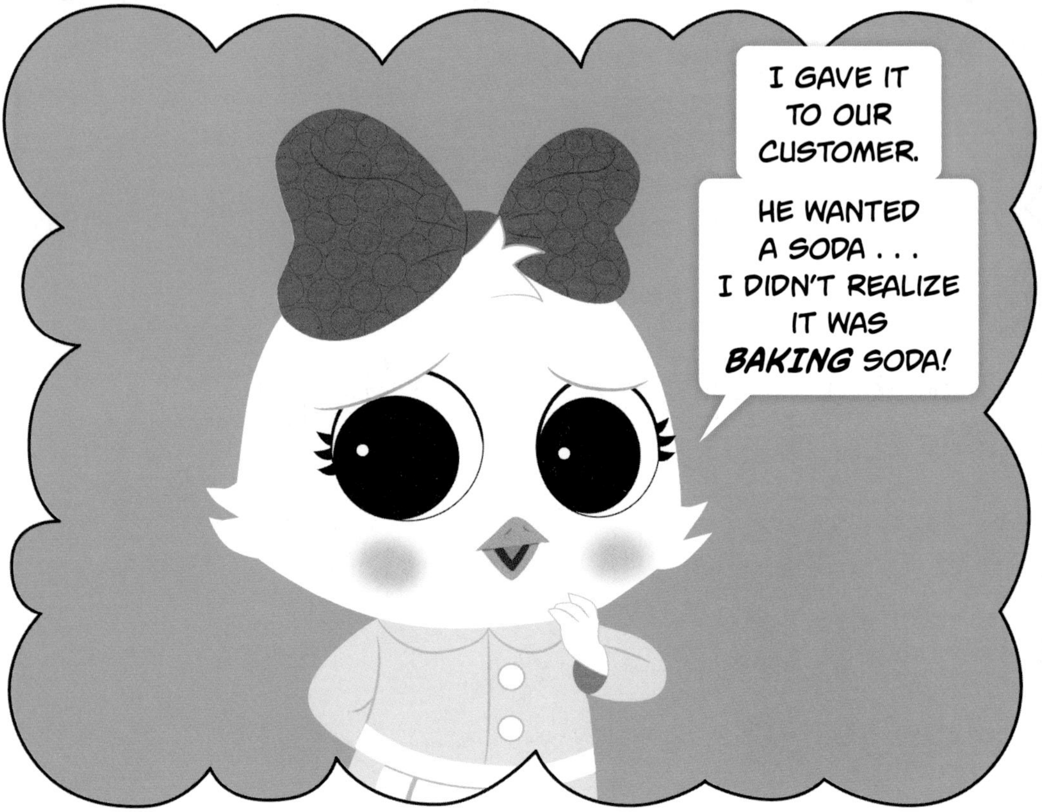
I GAVE IT TO OUR CUSTOMER.
HE WANTED A SODA . . . I DIDN'T REALIZE IT WAS *BAKING* SODA!

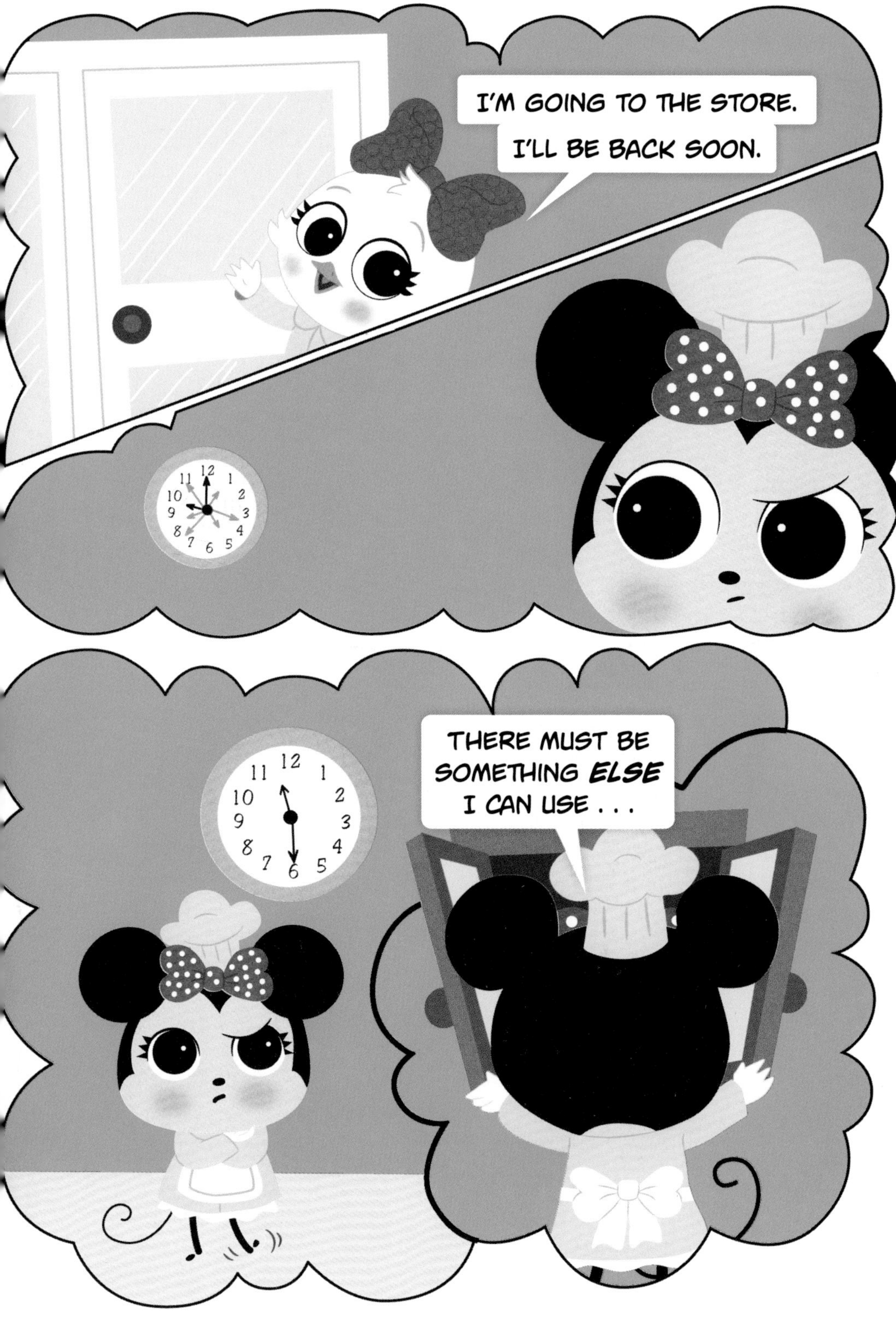
I'M GOING TO THE STORE.
I'LL BE BACK SOON.
THERE MUST BE SOMETHING *ELSE* I CAN USE . . .

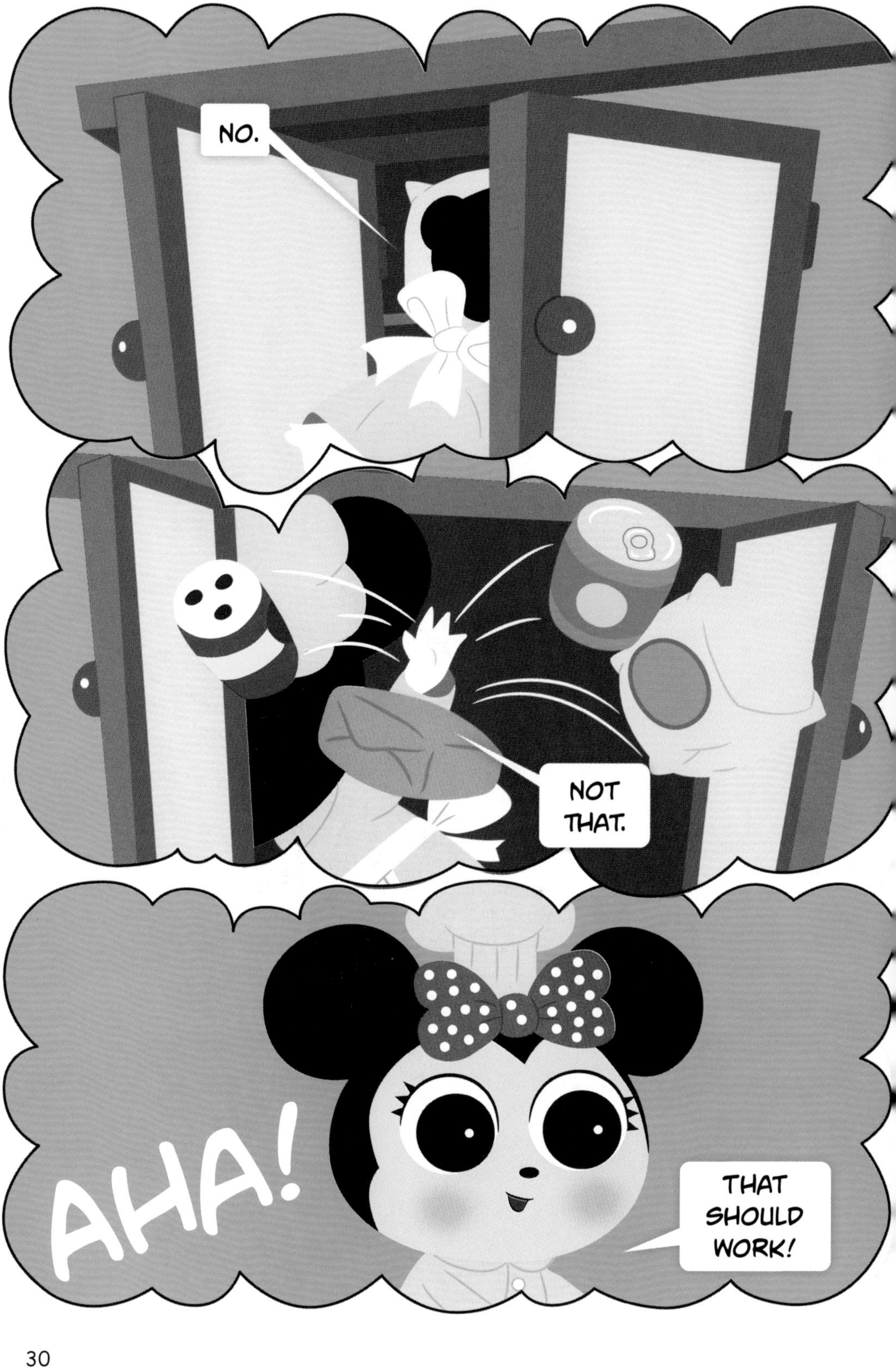
NO.
NOT THAT.
AHA!
THAT SHOULD WORK!

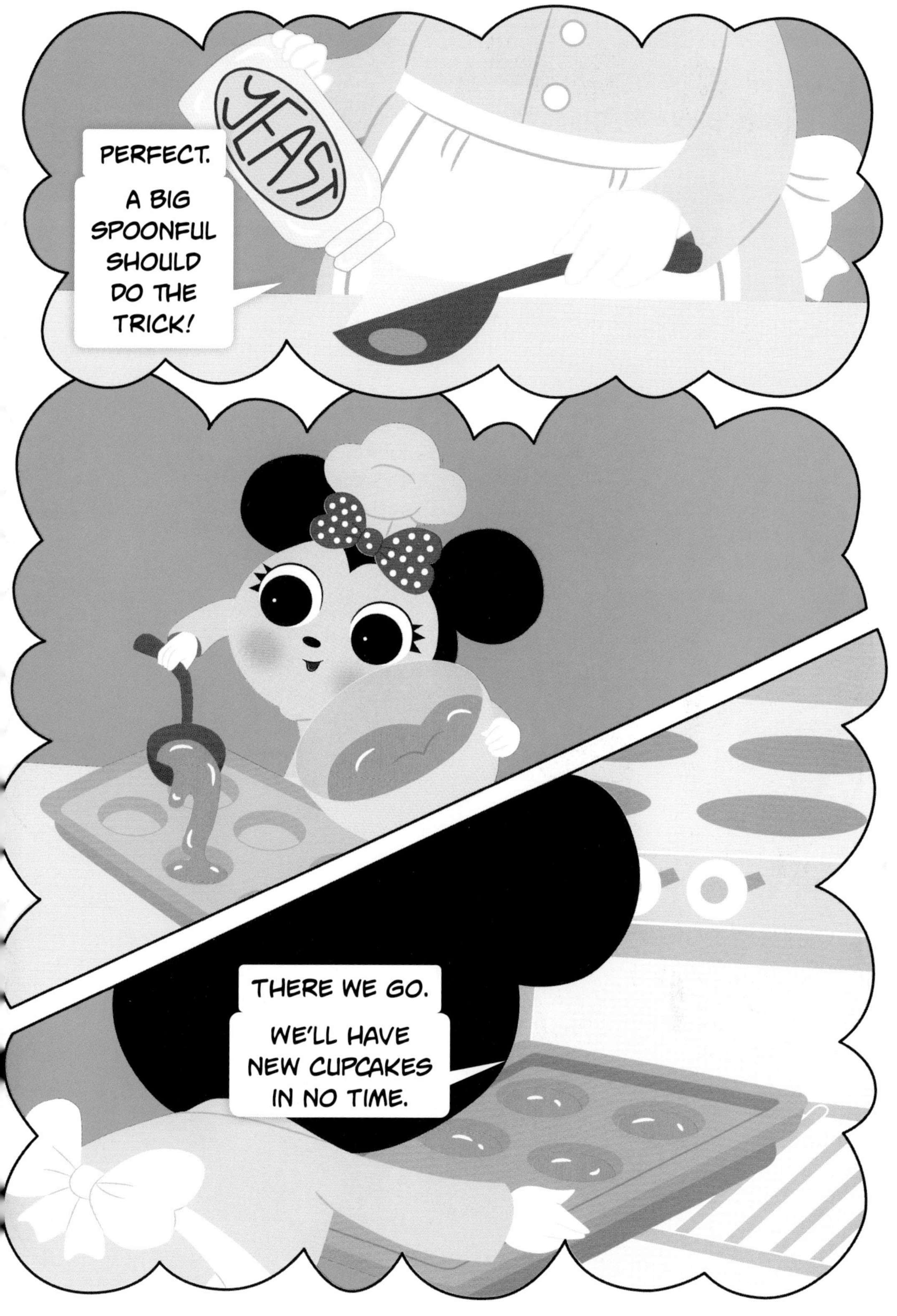
YEAST
PERFECT.
A BIG SPOONFUL SHOULD DO THE TRICK!
THERE WE GO.
WE'LL HAVE NEW CUPCAKES IN NO TIME.

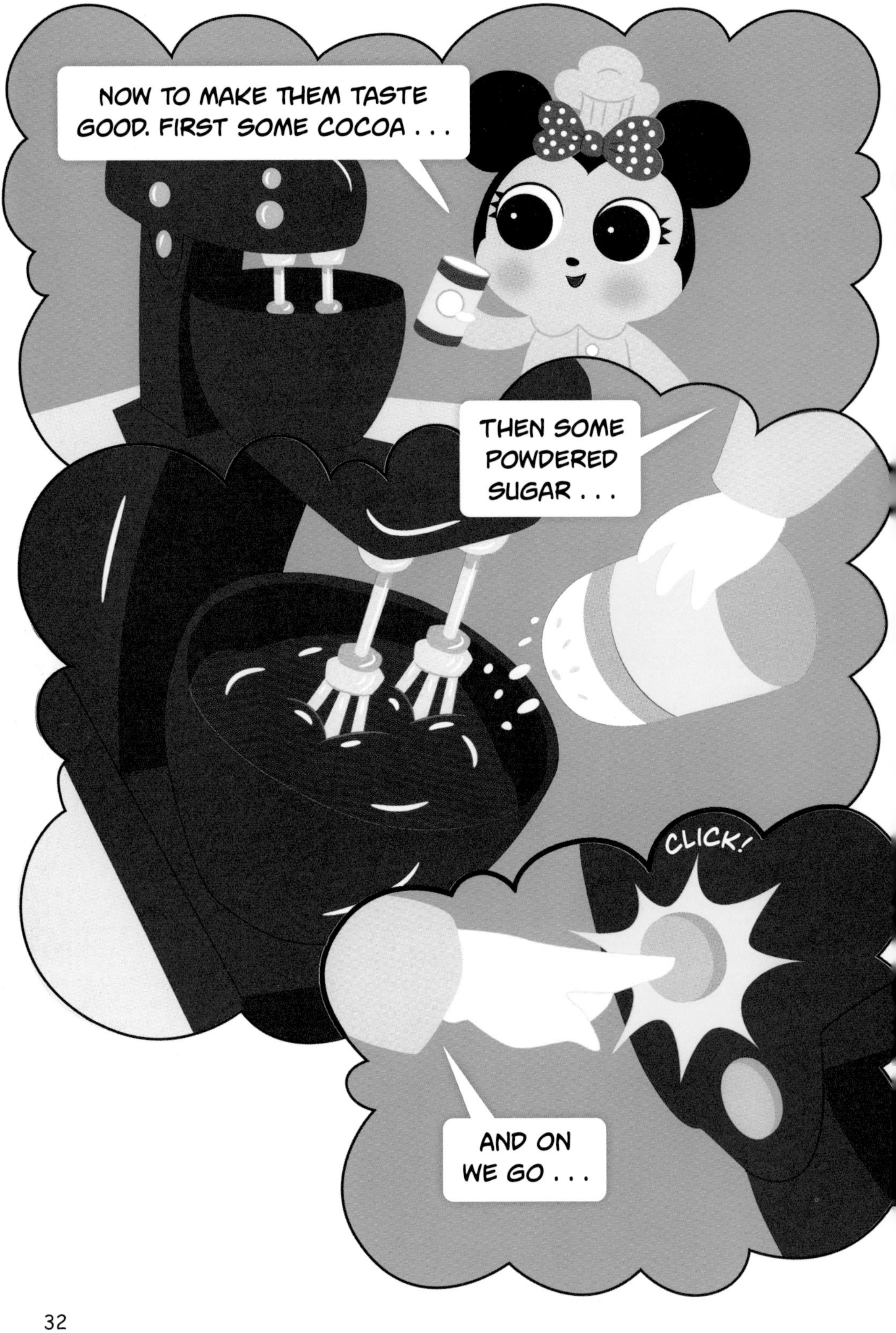
NOW TO MAKE THEM TASTE GOOD. FIRST SOME COCOA . . .
THEN SOME POWDERED SUGAR . . .
CLICK!
AND ON WE GO . . .

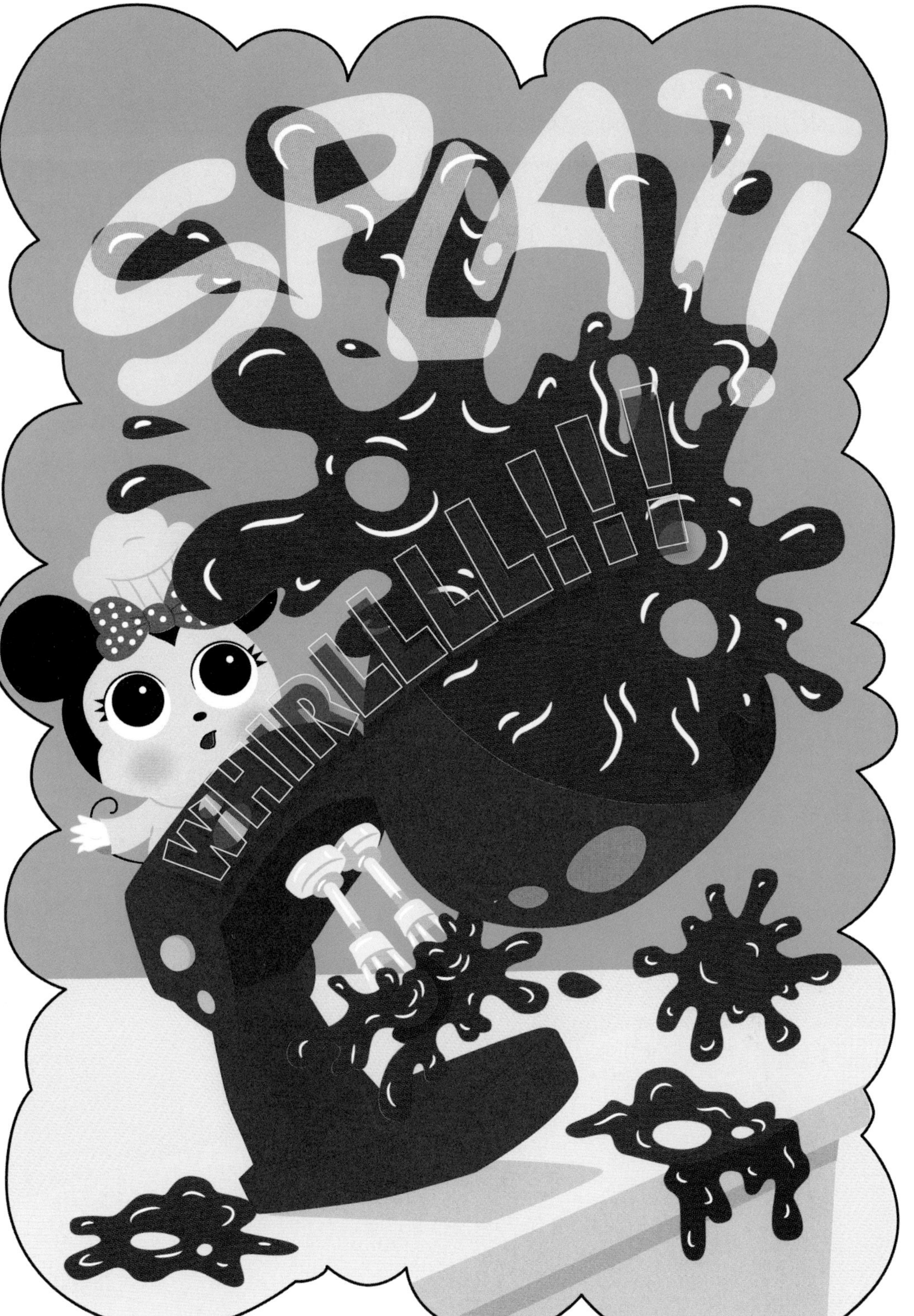
SPLAT!
WHIRLLL!!!

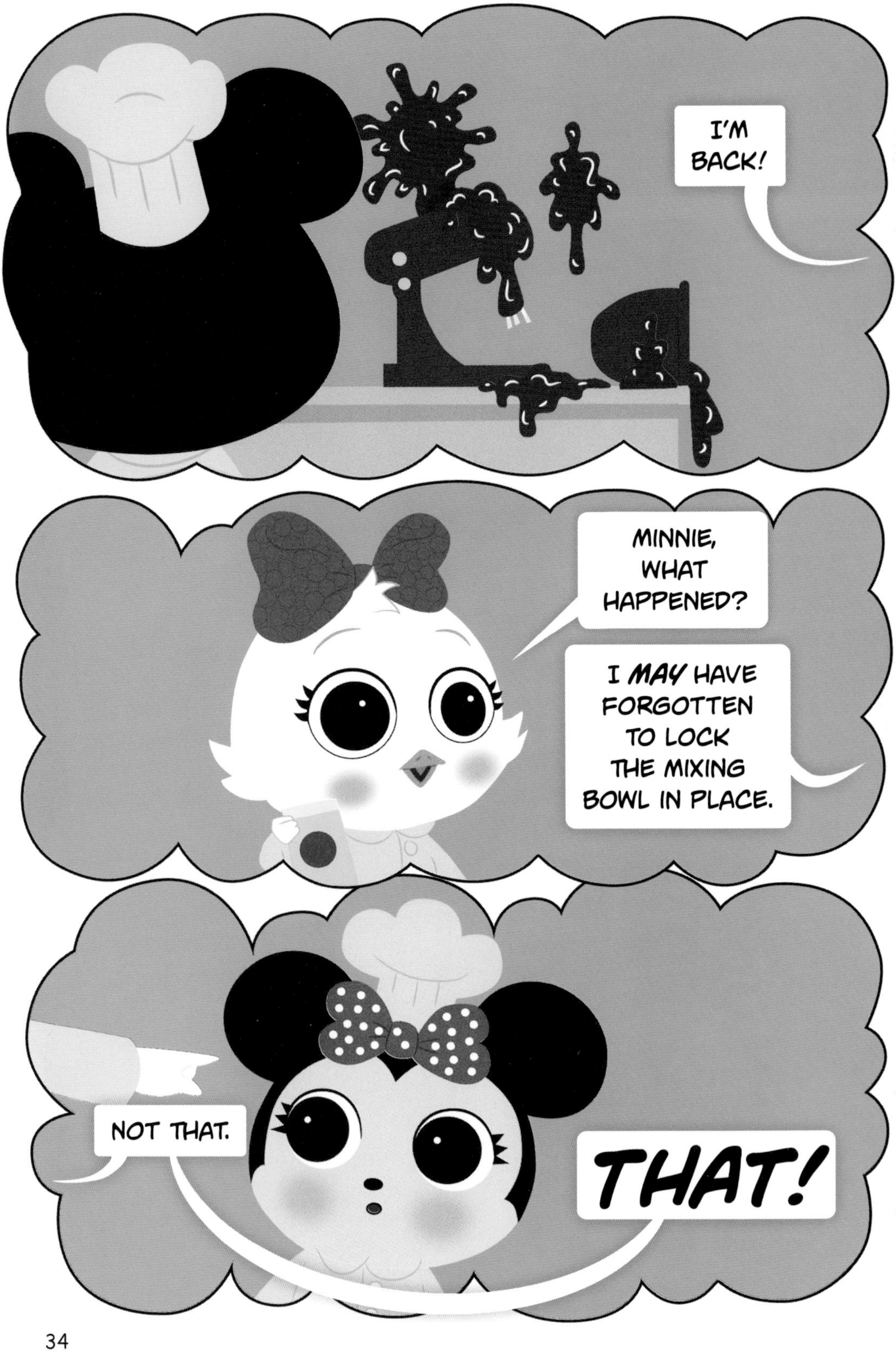
I'M BACK!
MINNIE, WHAT HAPPENED?
I MAY HAVE FORGOTTEN TO LOCK THE MIXING BOWL IN PLACE.
NOT THAT.
THAT!

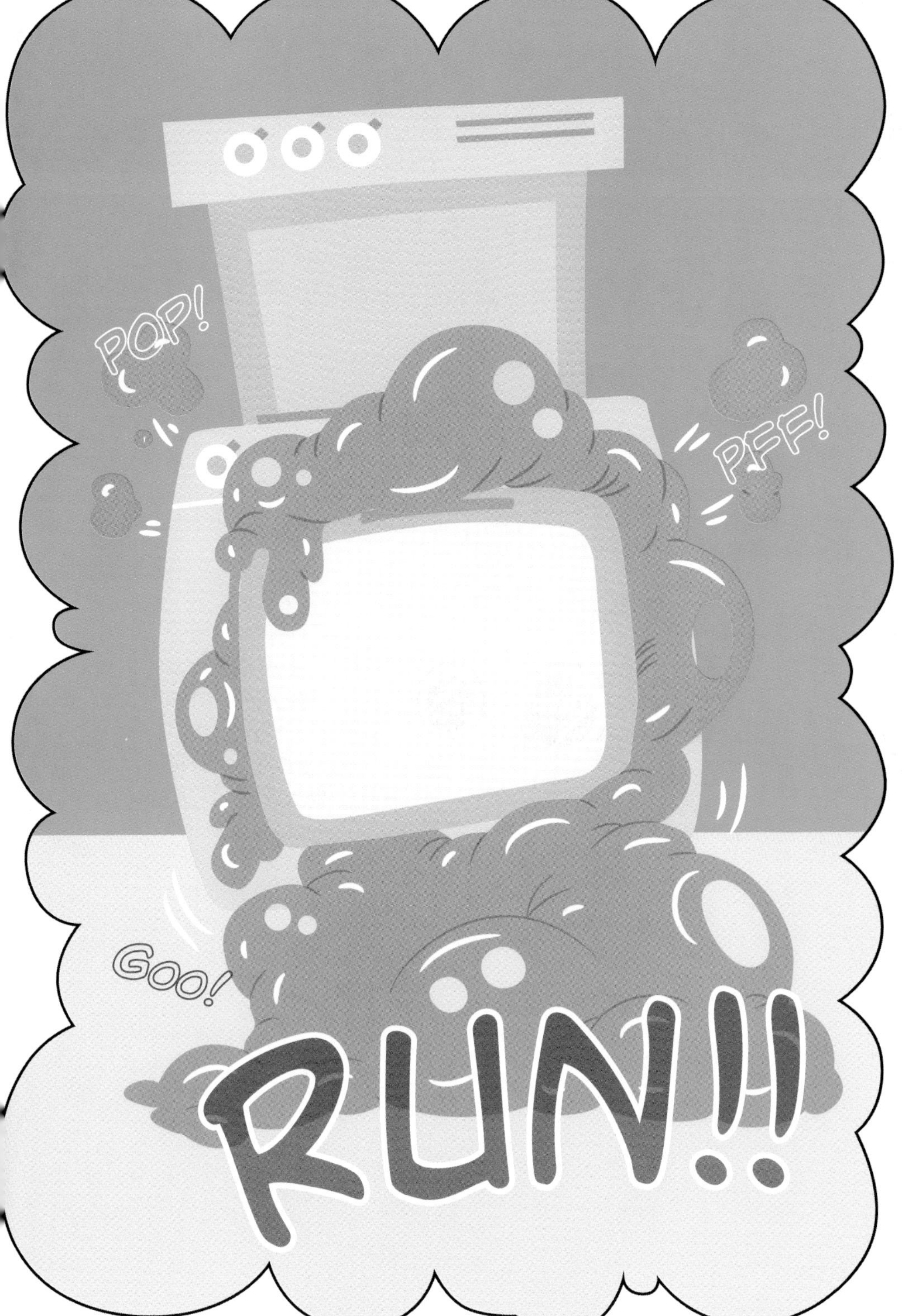
POP!
PFF!
GOO!
RUN!!

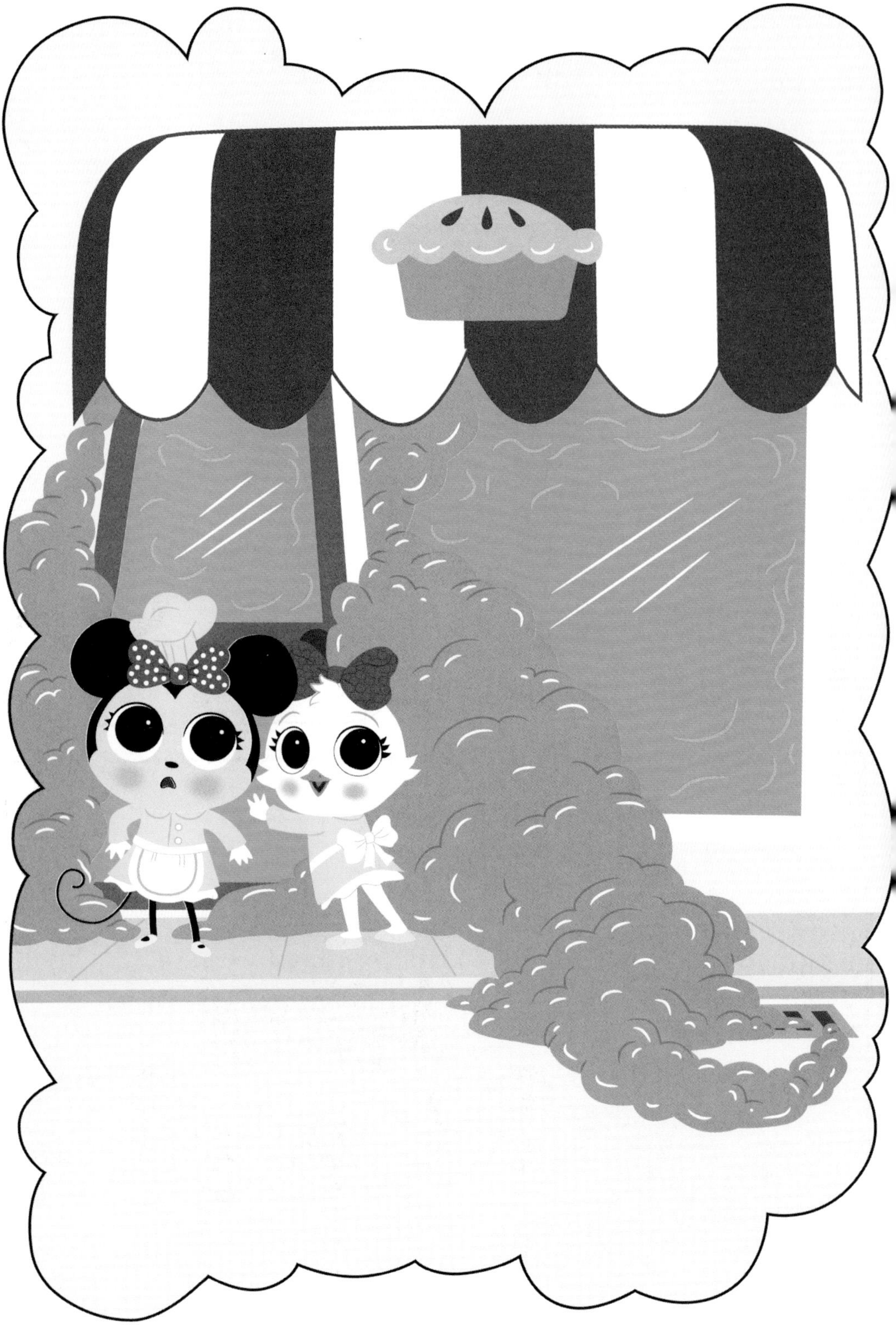

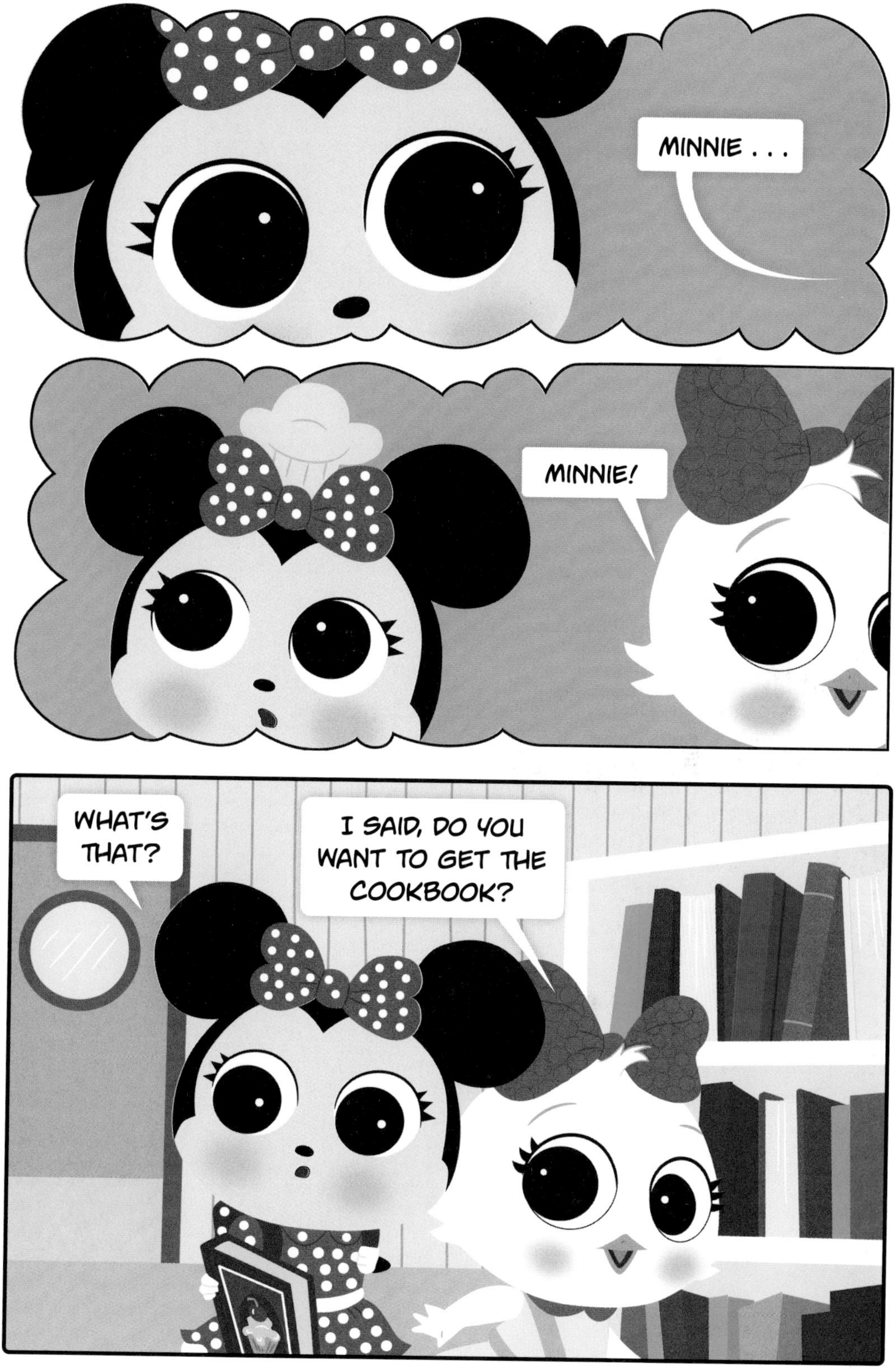
MINNIE . . .
MINNIE!
WHAT'S THAT?
I SAID, DO YOU WANT TO GET THE COOKBOOK?

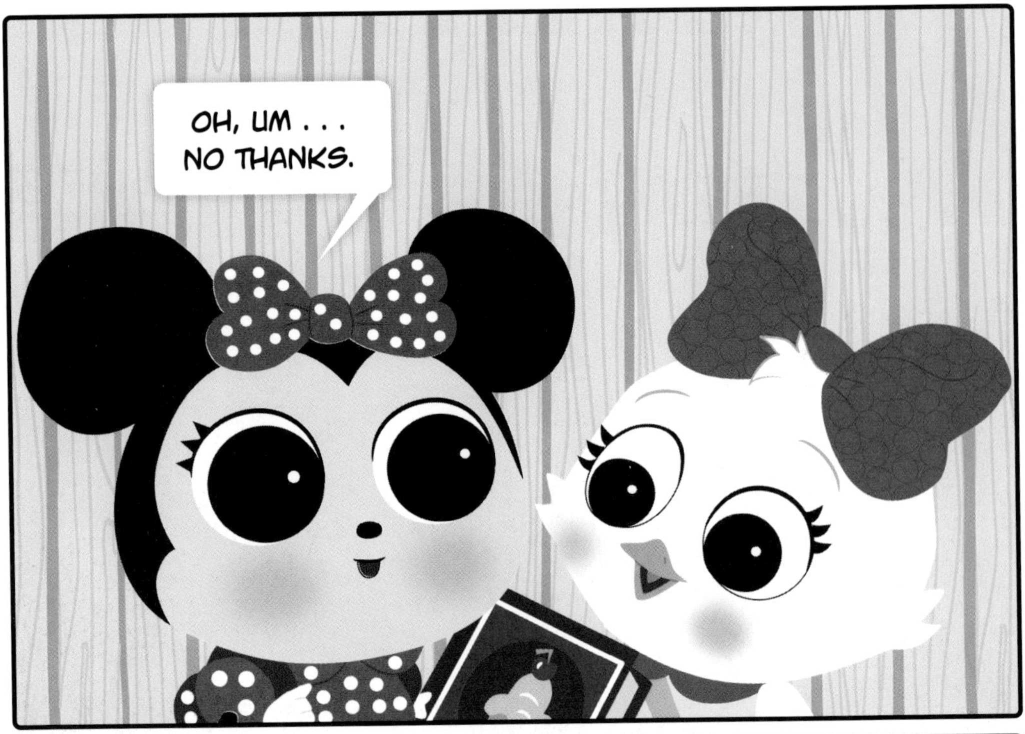
OH, UM . . .
NO THANKS.

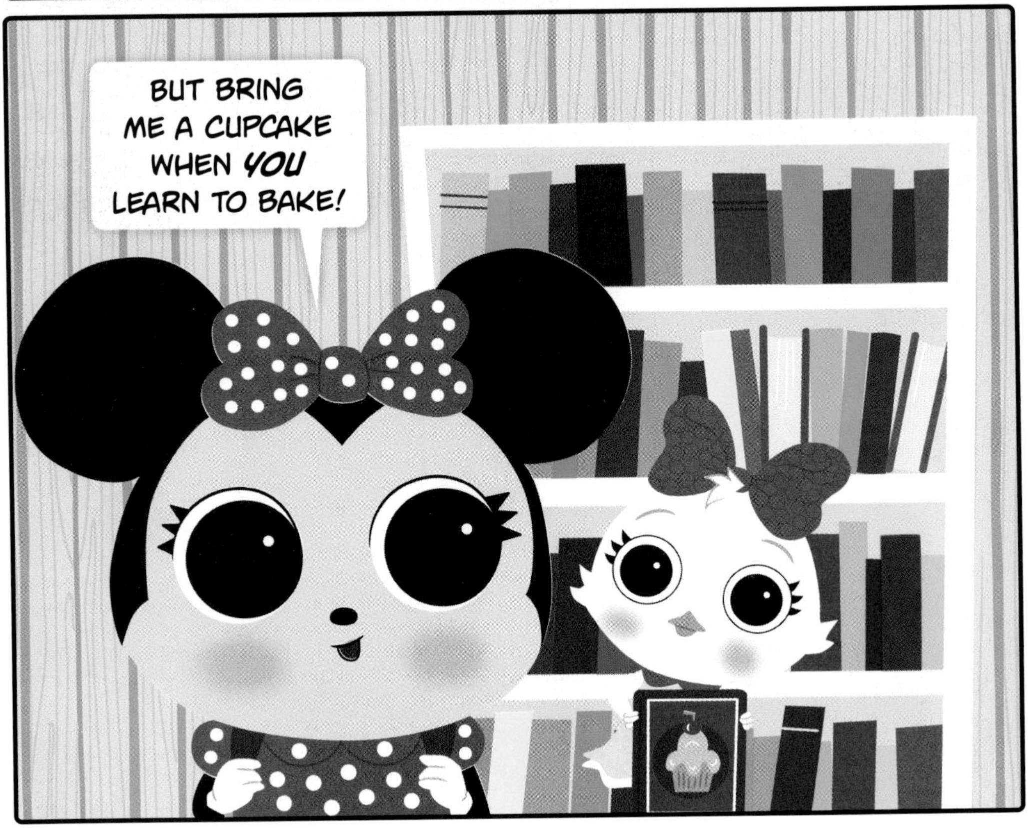
BUT BRING ME A CUPCAKE WHEN YOU LEARN TO BAKE!

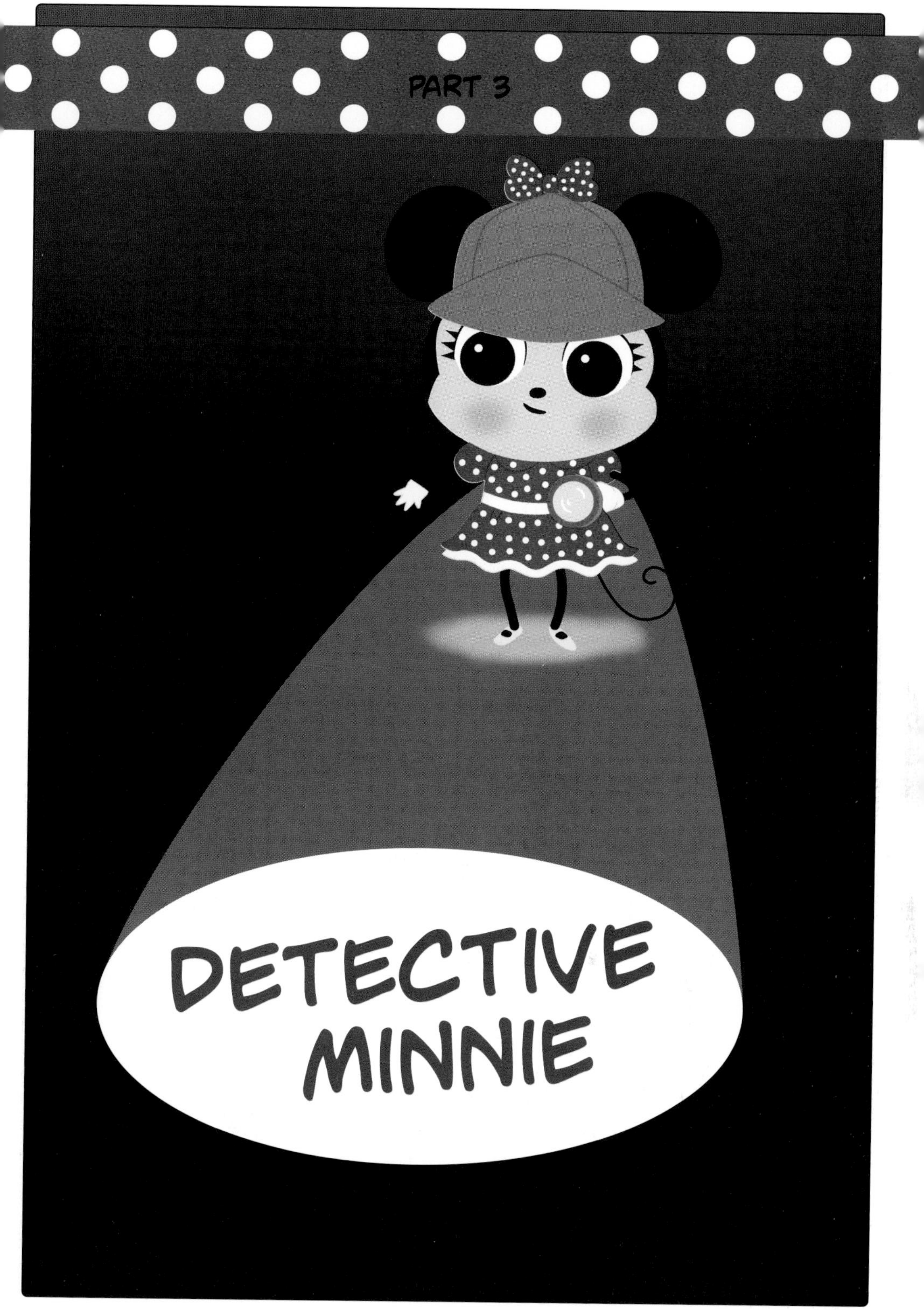
PART 3
DETECTIVE MINNIE

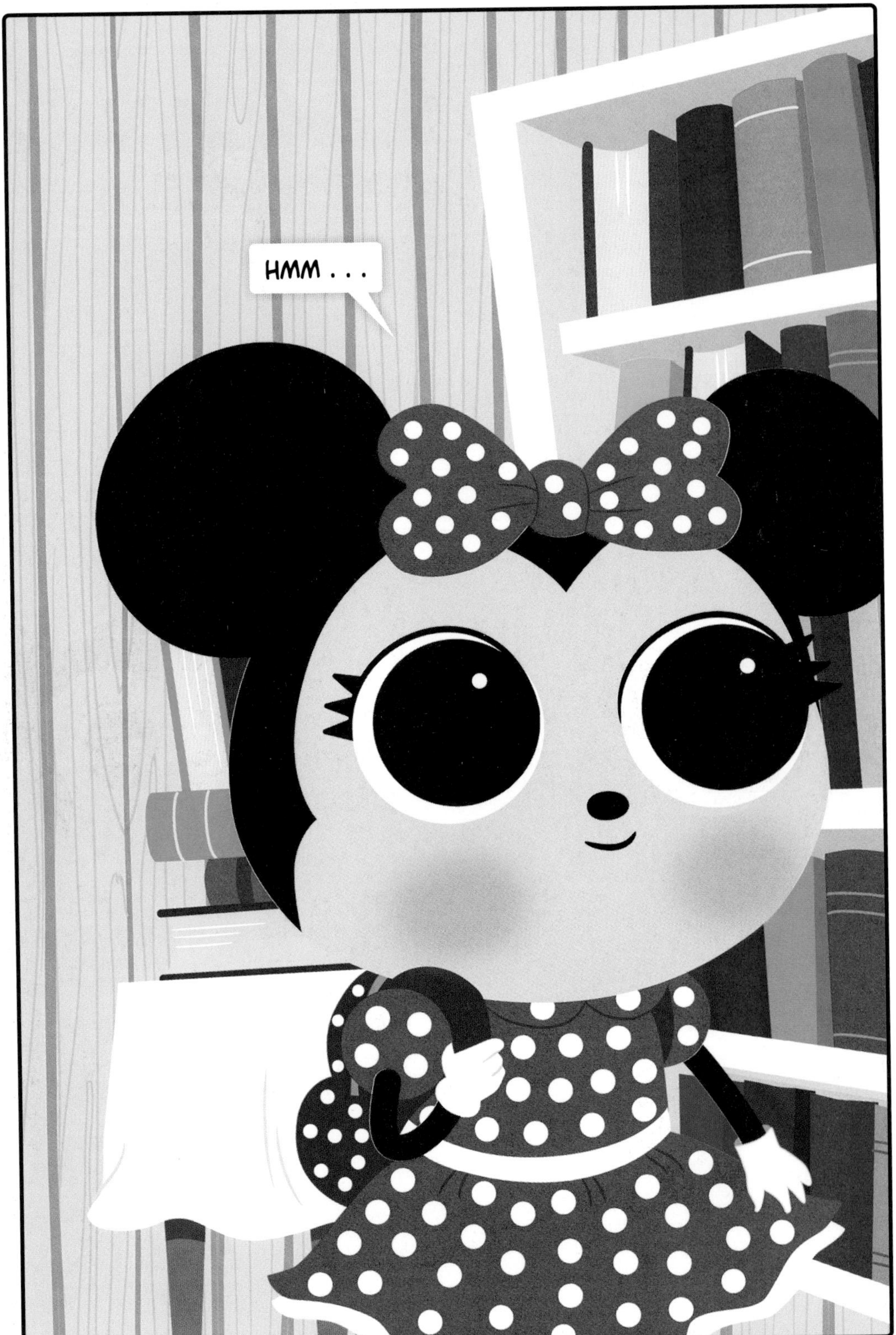
HMM . . .

MAYBE . . .

BUMP!

OUCH!

SORRY, MICKEY.

I DIDN'T SEE YOU THERE!

THAT'S OKAY, MINNIE.

SAY, DID YOU PICK A BOOK YET?

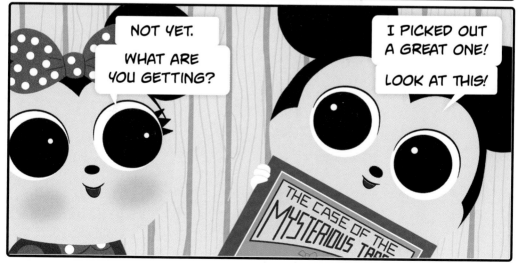

NOT YET.

WHAT ARE YOU GETTING?

I PICKED OUT A GREAT ONE!

LOOK AT THIS!

THE CASE OF THE MYSTERIOUS TREE

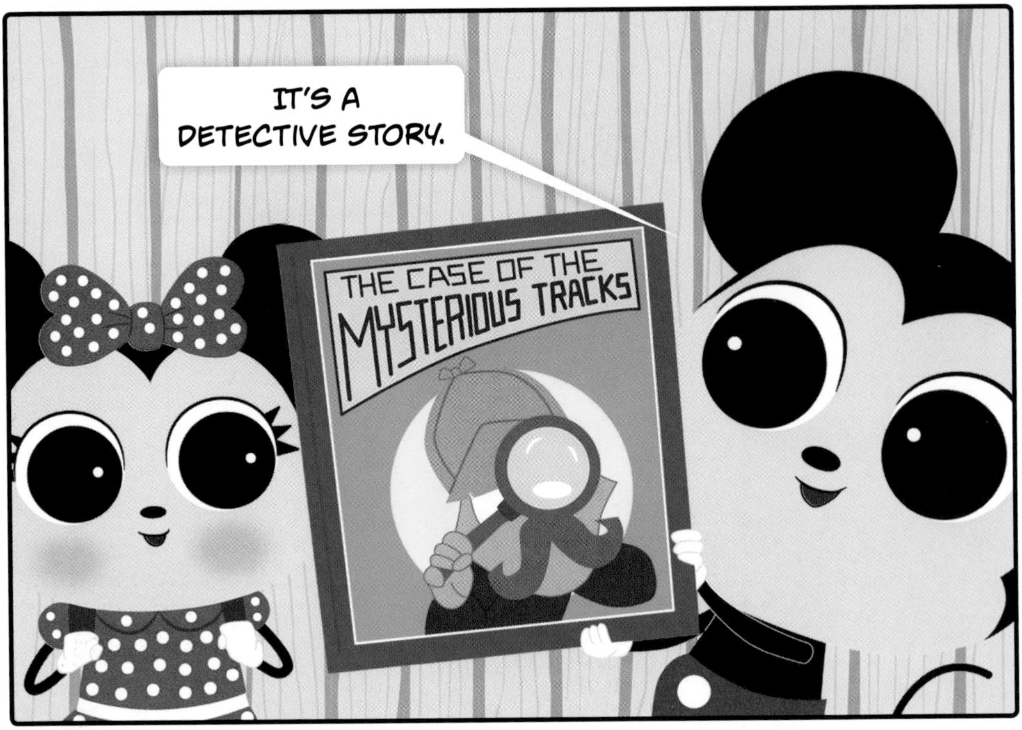
IT'S A DETECTIVE STORY.
THE CASE OF THE MYSTERIOUS TRACKS

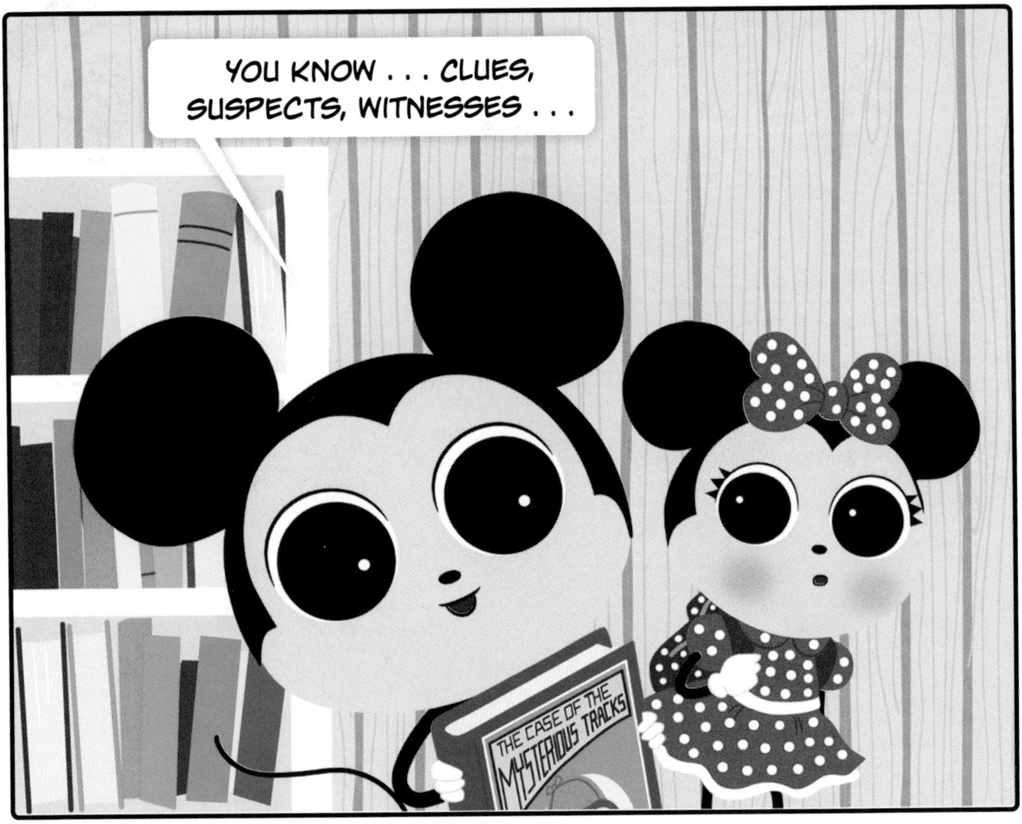
YOU KNOW . . . CLUES, SUSPECTS, WITNESSES . . .
THE CASE OF THE MYSTERIOUS TRACKS

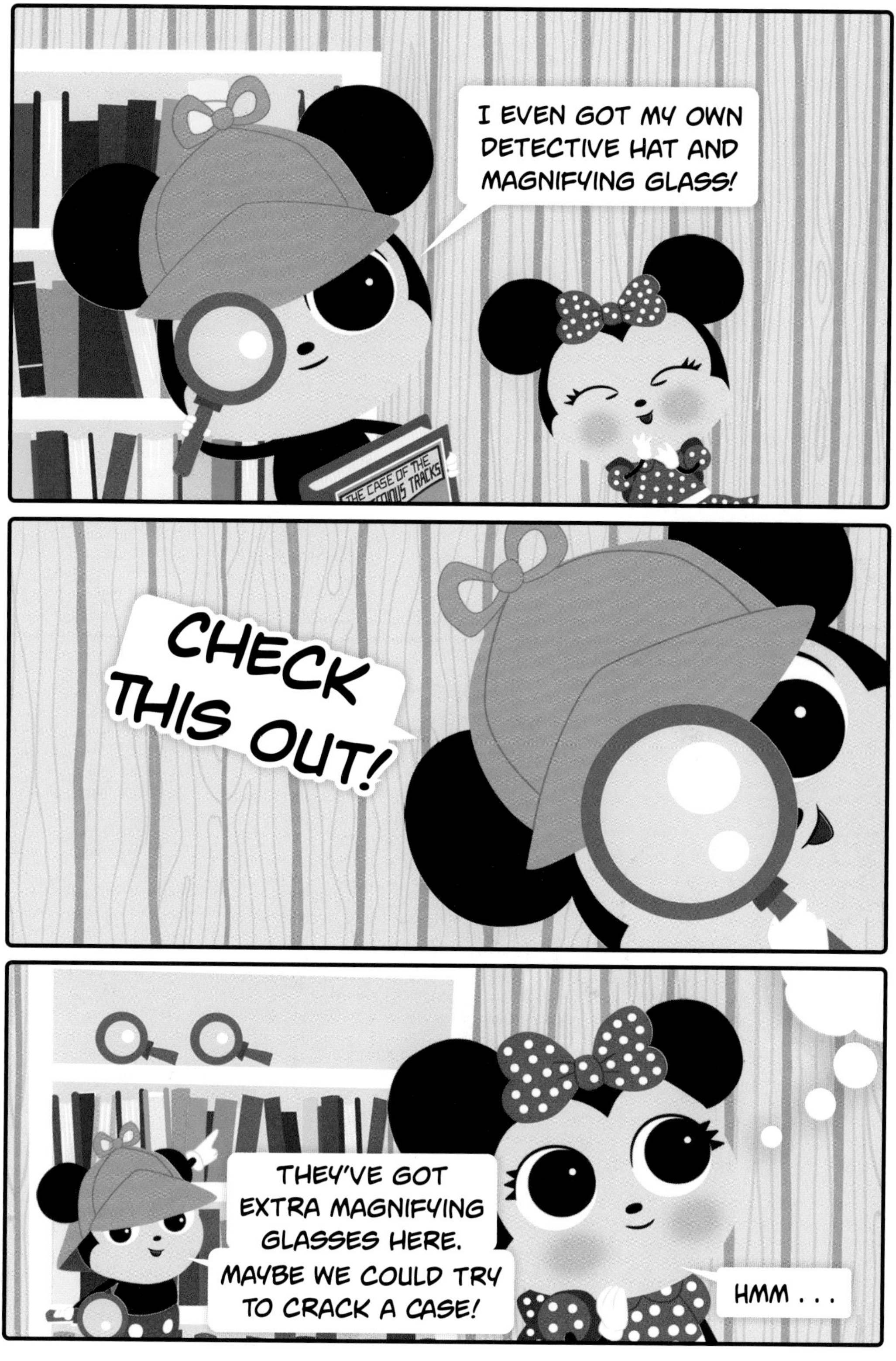
I EVEN GOT MY OWN DETECTIVE HAT AND MAGNIFYING GLASS!
THE CASE OF THE MYSTERIOUS TRACKS
CHECK THIS OUT!
THEY'VE GOT EXTRA MAGNIFYING GLASSES HERE.
MAYBE WE COULD TRY TO CRACK A CASE!
HMM . . .

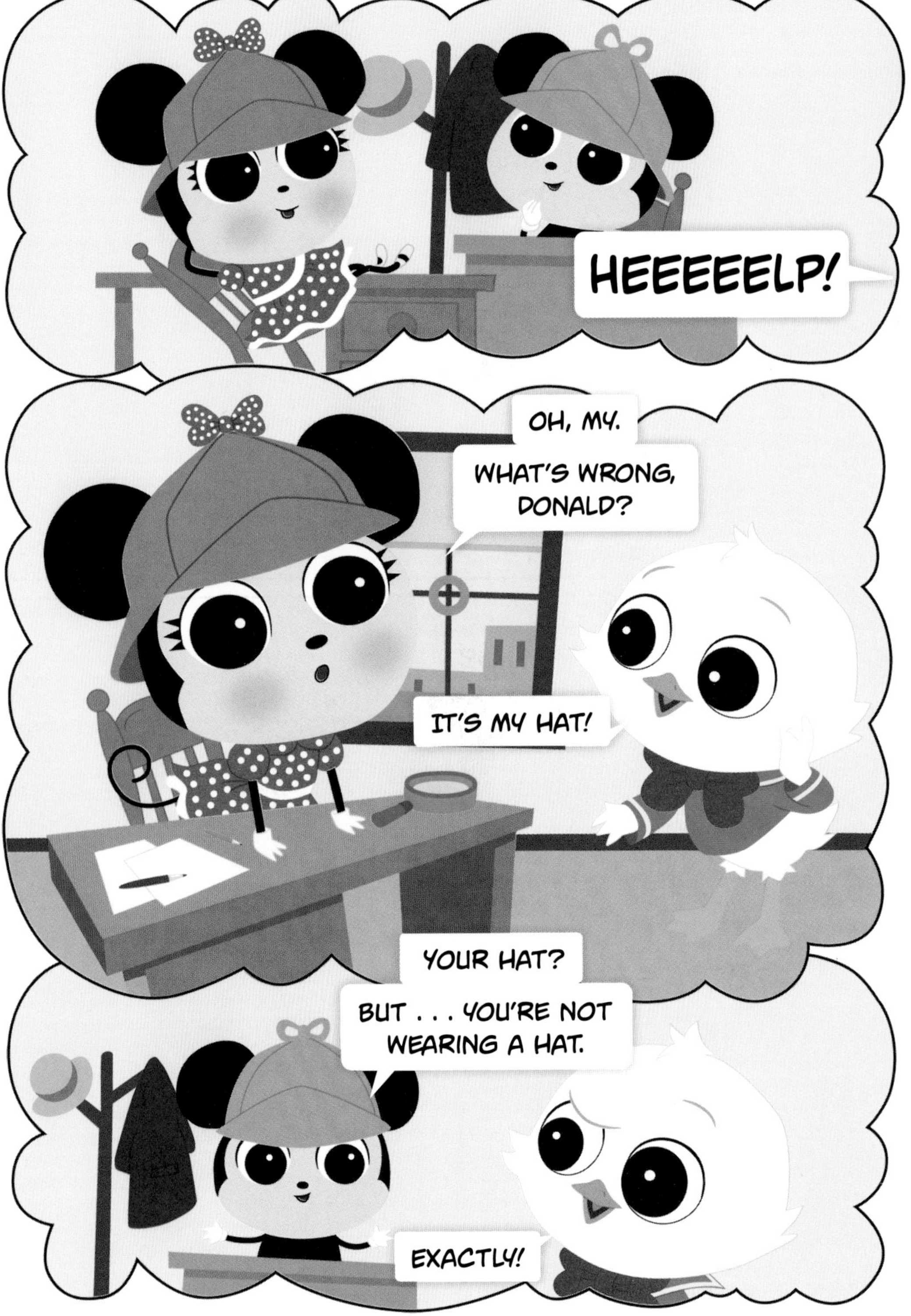
HEEEEEELP!
OH, MY.
WHAT'S WRONG, DONALD?
IT'S MY HAT!
YOUR HAT?
BUT . . . YOU'RE NOT WEARING A HAT.
EXACTLY!

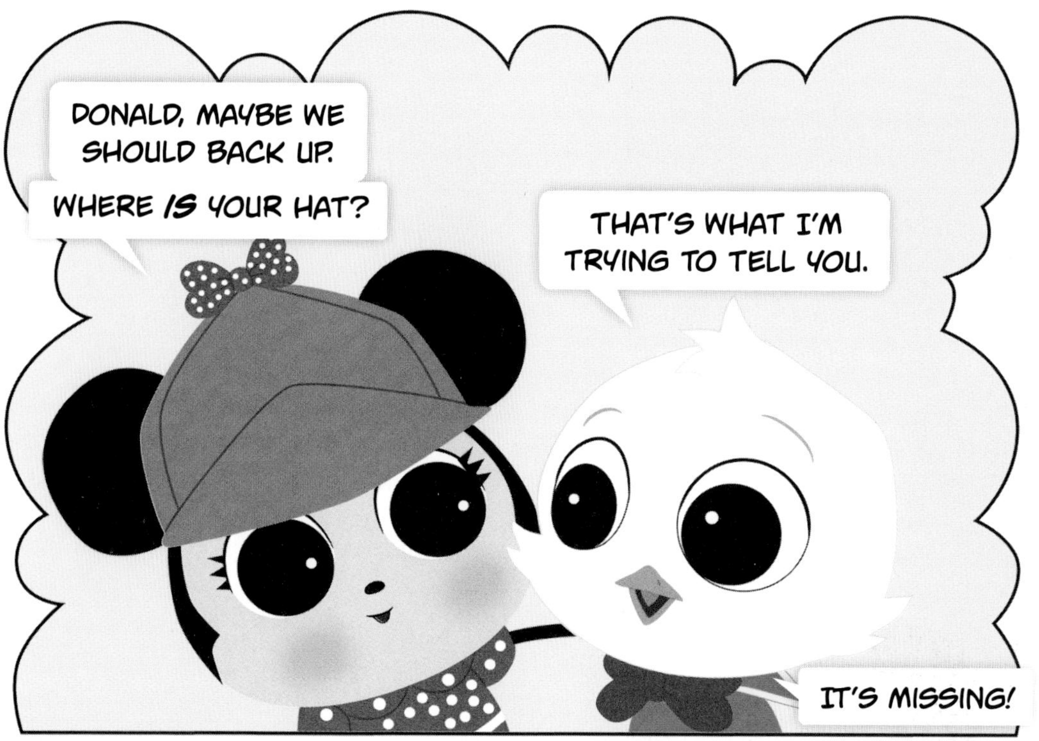
DONALD, MAYBE WE SHOULD BACK UP.
WHERE *IS* YOUR HAT?
THAT'S WHAT I'M TRYING TO TELL YOU.
IT'S MISSING!

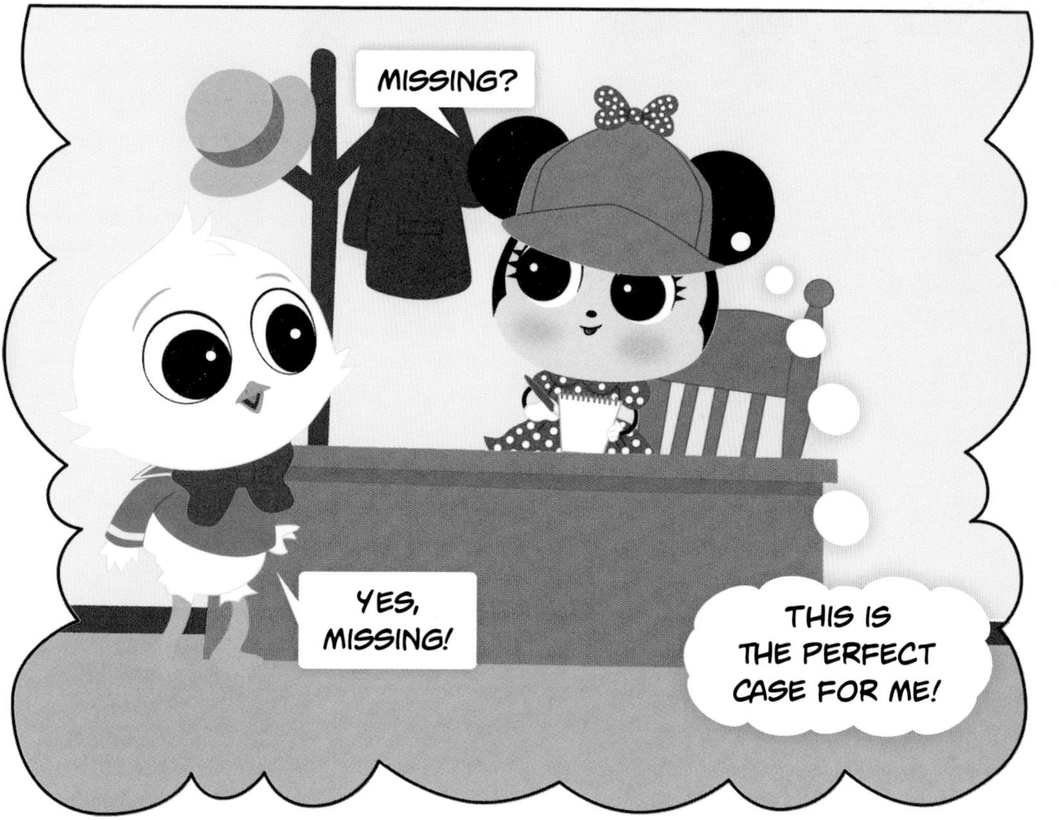
MISSING?
YES, MISSING!
THIS IS THE PERFECT CASE FOR ME!

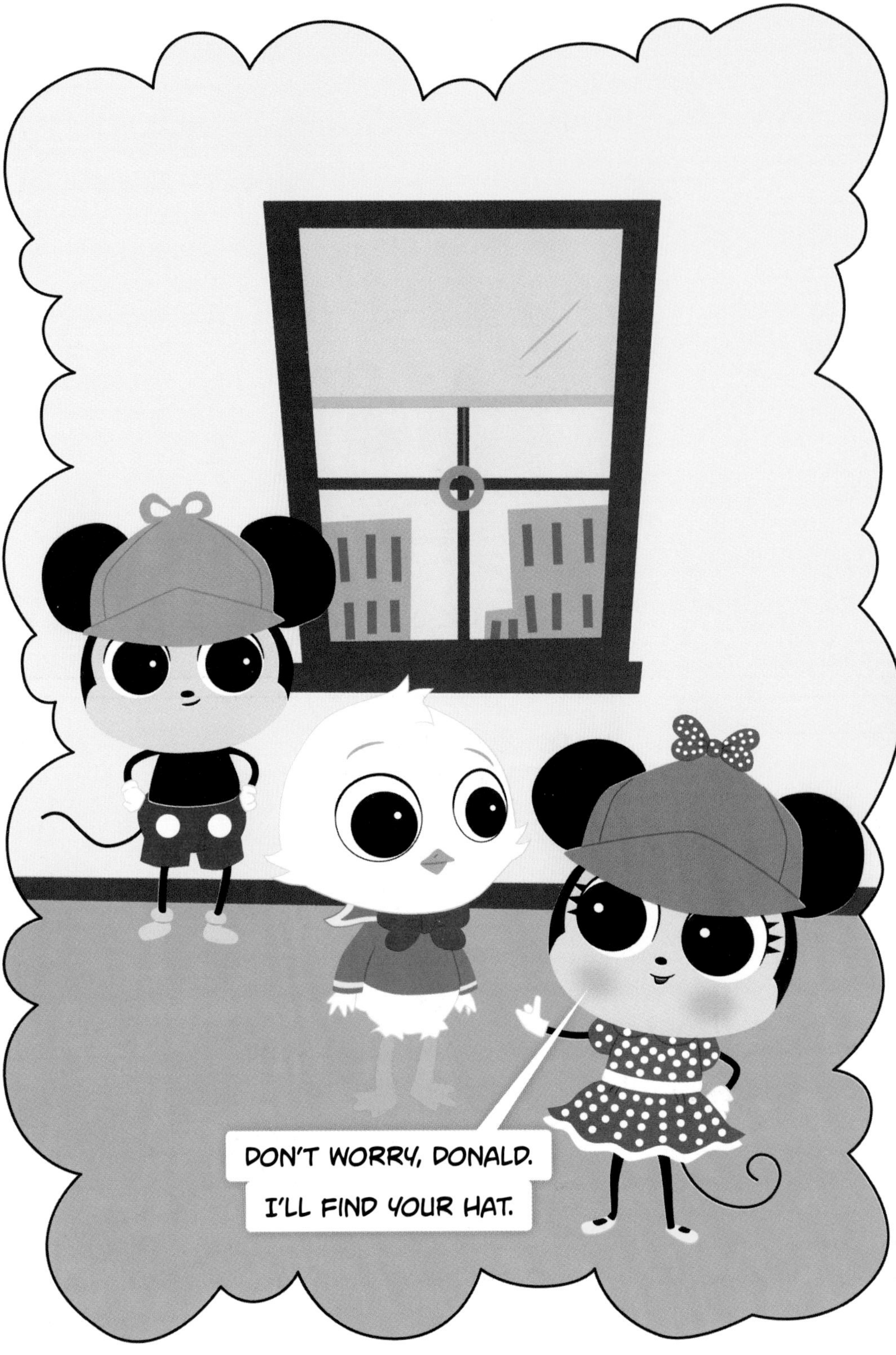
DON'T WORRY, DONALD.
I'LL FIND YOUR HAT.

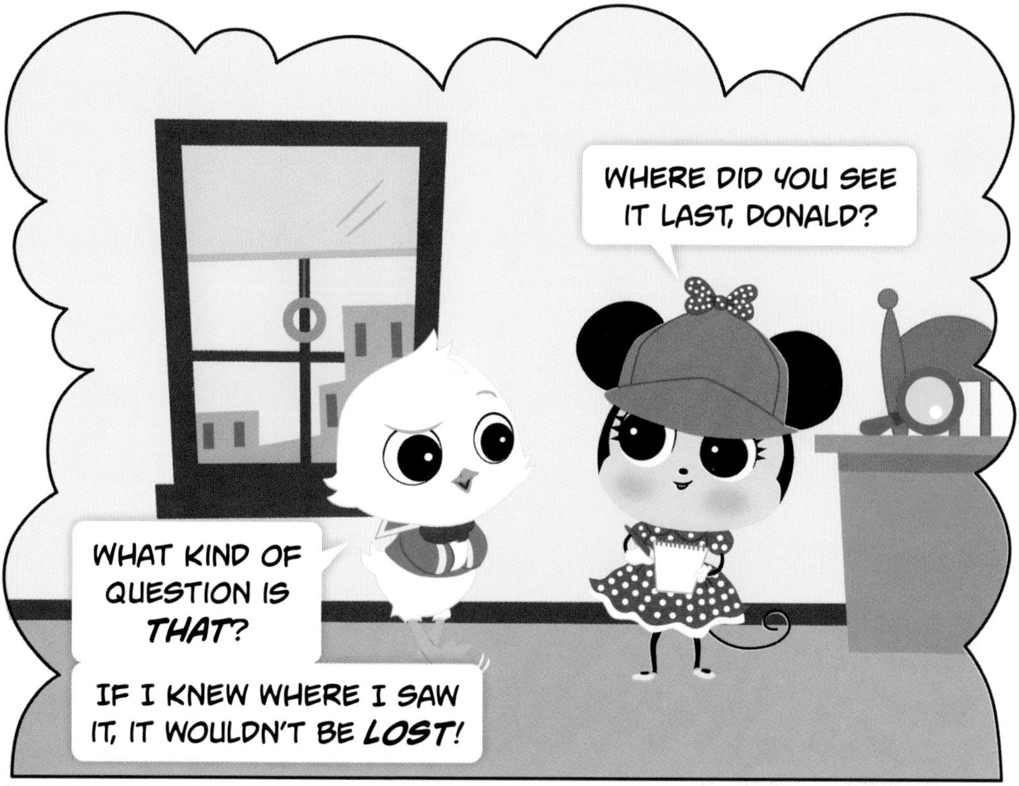
WHERE DID YOU SEE IT LAST, DONALD?
WHAT KIND OF QUESTION IS *THAT*?
IF I KNEW WHERE I SAW IT, IT WOULDN'T BE *LOST*!

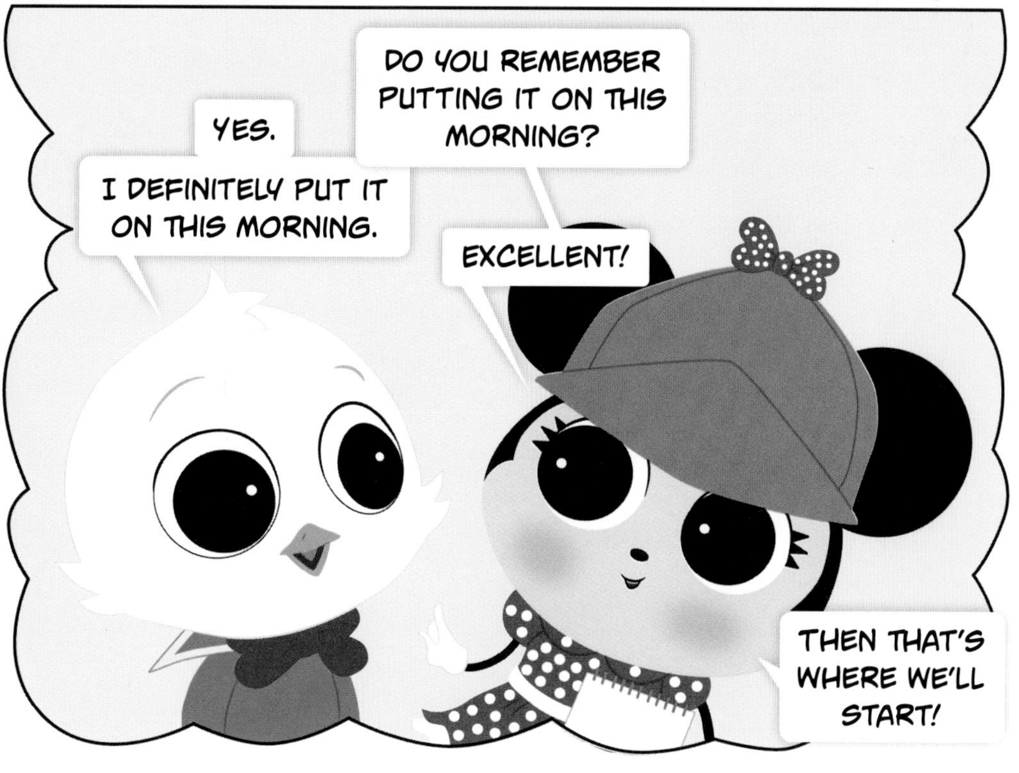
DO YOU REMEMBER PUTTING IT ON THIS MORNING?
YES.
I DEFINITELY PUT IT ON THIS MORNING.
EXCELLENT!
THEN THAT'S WHERE WE'LL START!

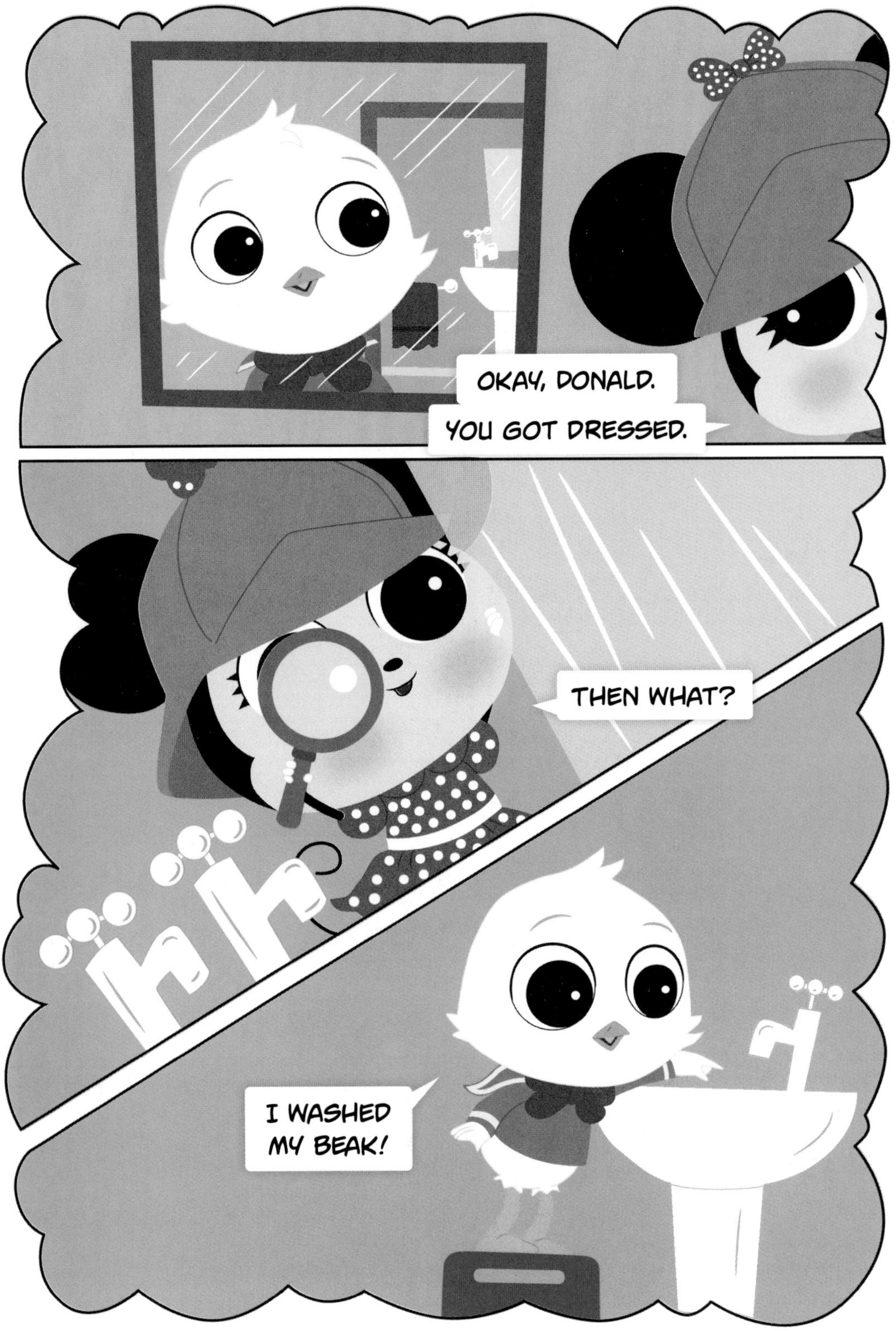
OKAY, DONALD.
YOU GOT DRESSED.
THEN WHAT?
I WASHED MY BEAK!

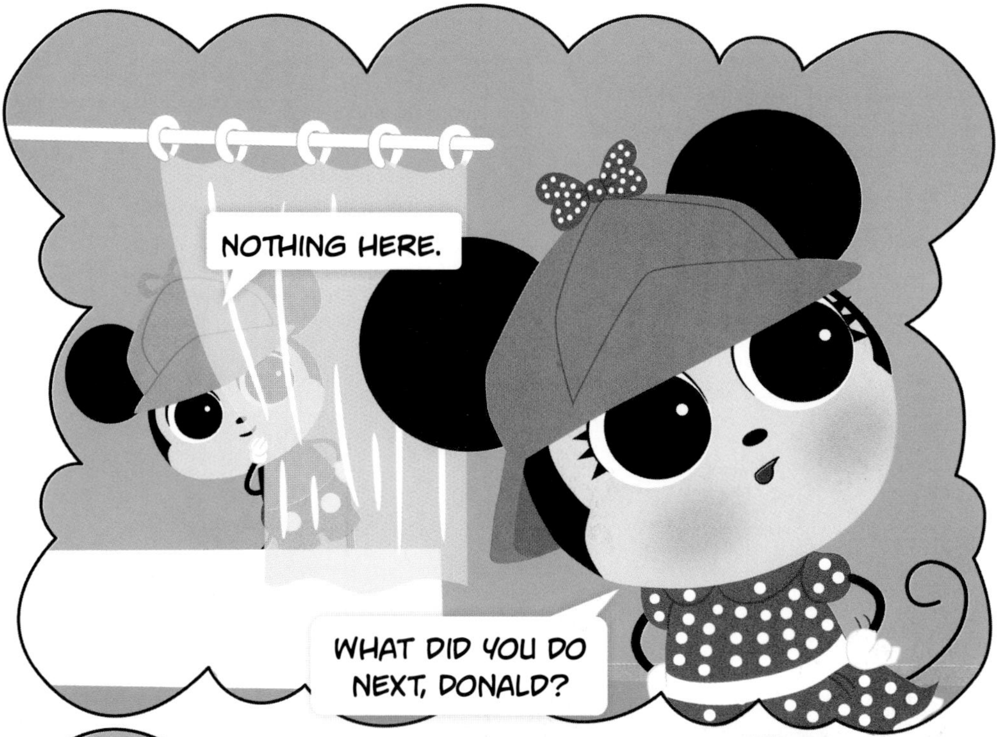
NOTHING HERE.
WHAT DID YOU DO NEXT, DONALD?

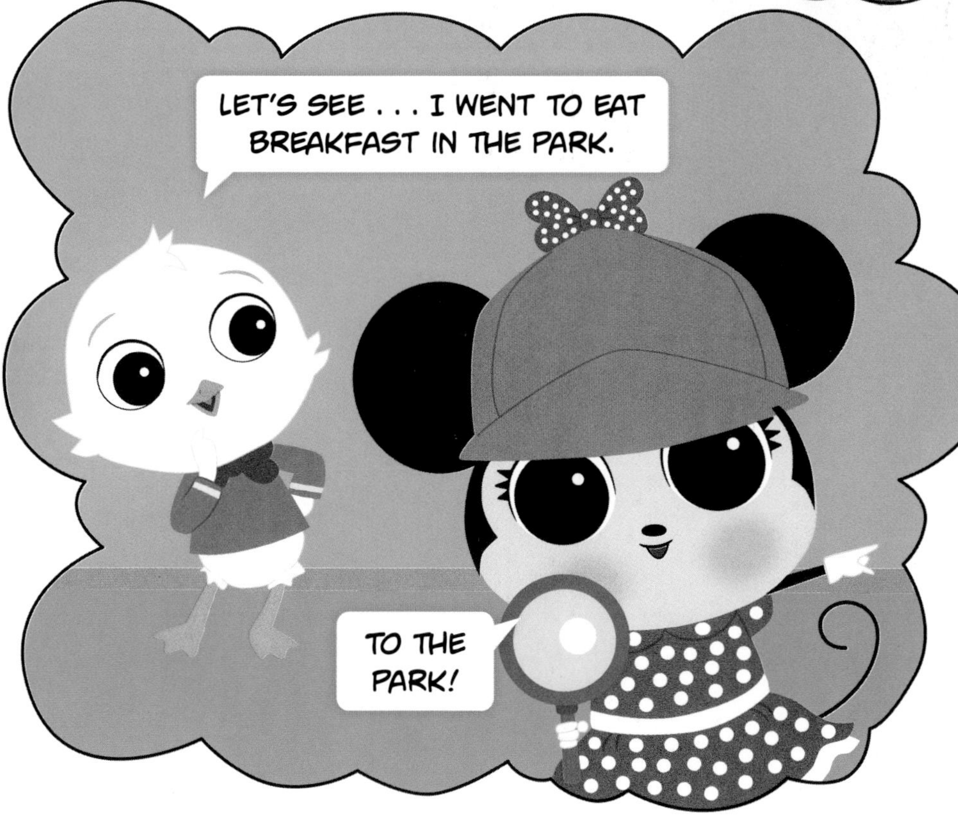
LET'S SEE . . . I WENT TO EAT BREAKFAST IN THE PARK.
TO THE PARK!

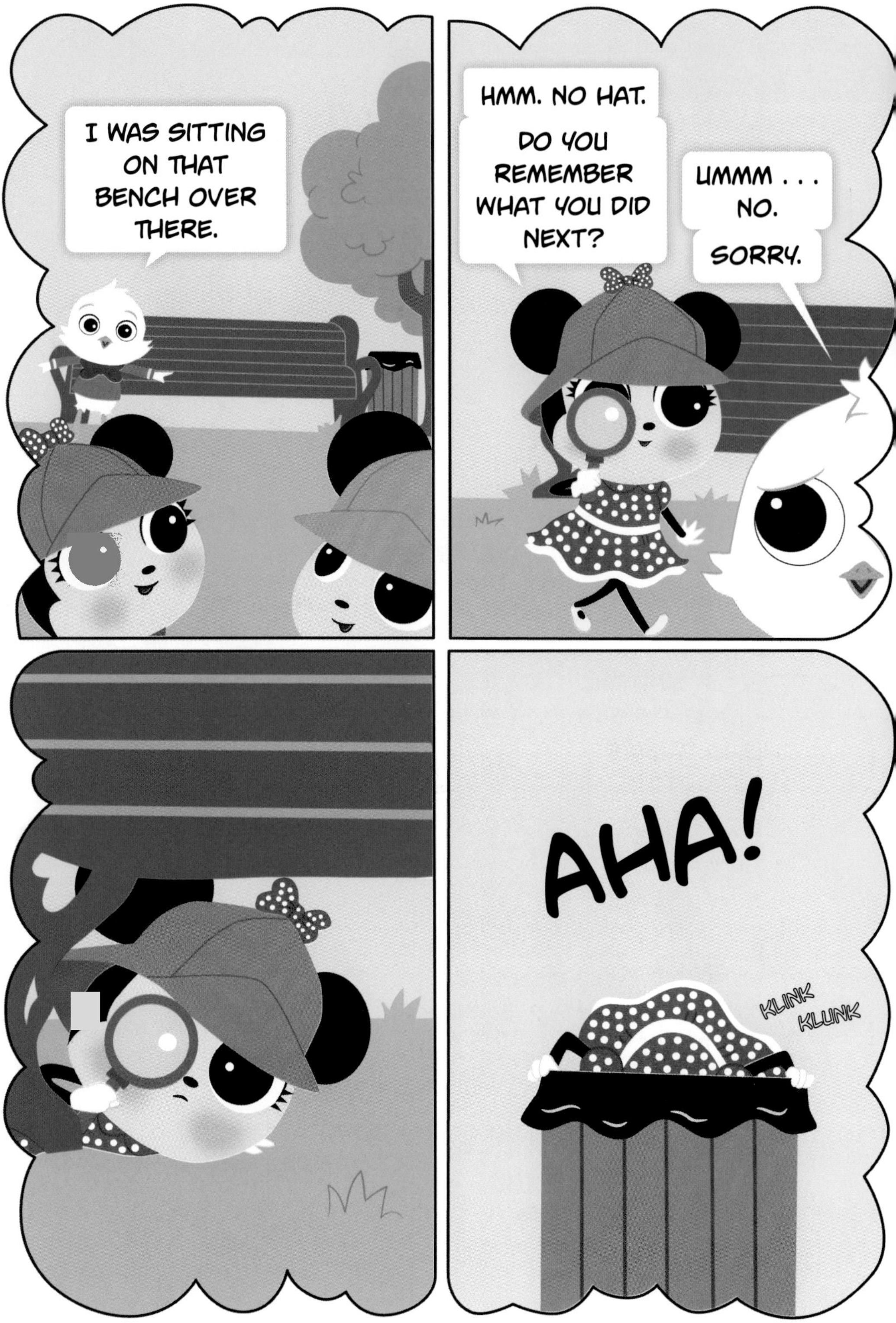

I WAS SITTING ON THAT BENCH OVER THERE.
HMM. NO HAT.
DO YOU REMEMBER WHAT YOU DID NEXT?
UMMM . . . NO.
SORRY.
AHA!
KLINK
KLUNK

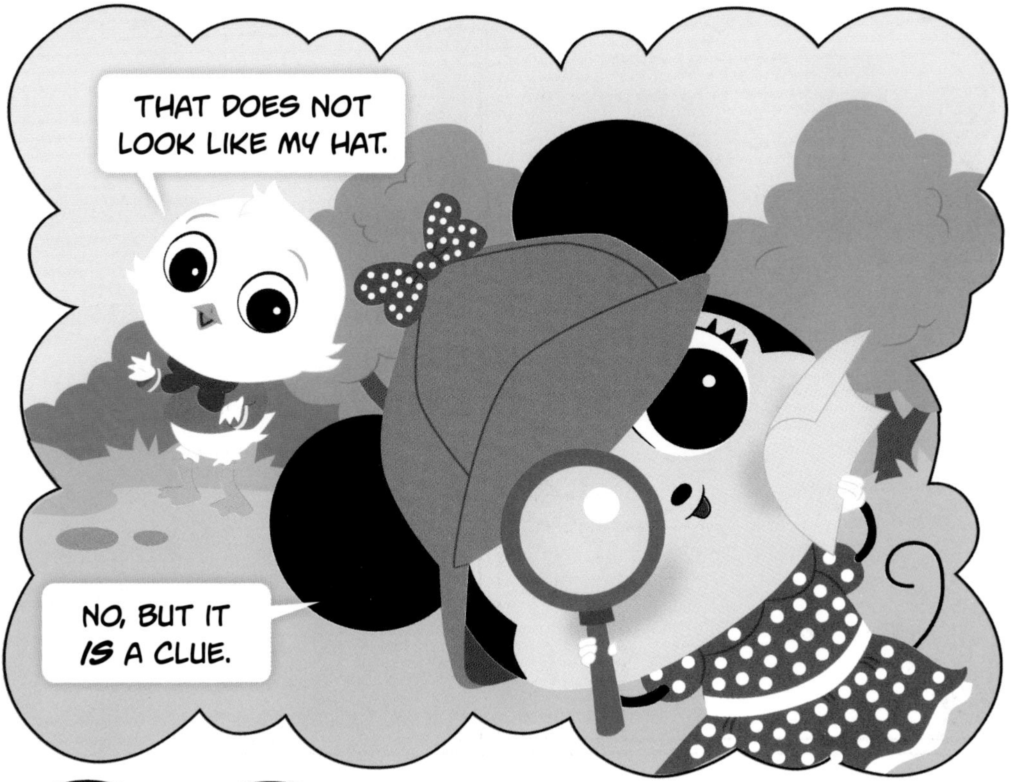
THAT DOES NOT LOOK LIKE MY HAT.
NO, BUT IT *IS* A CLUE.

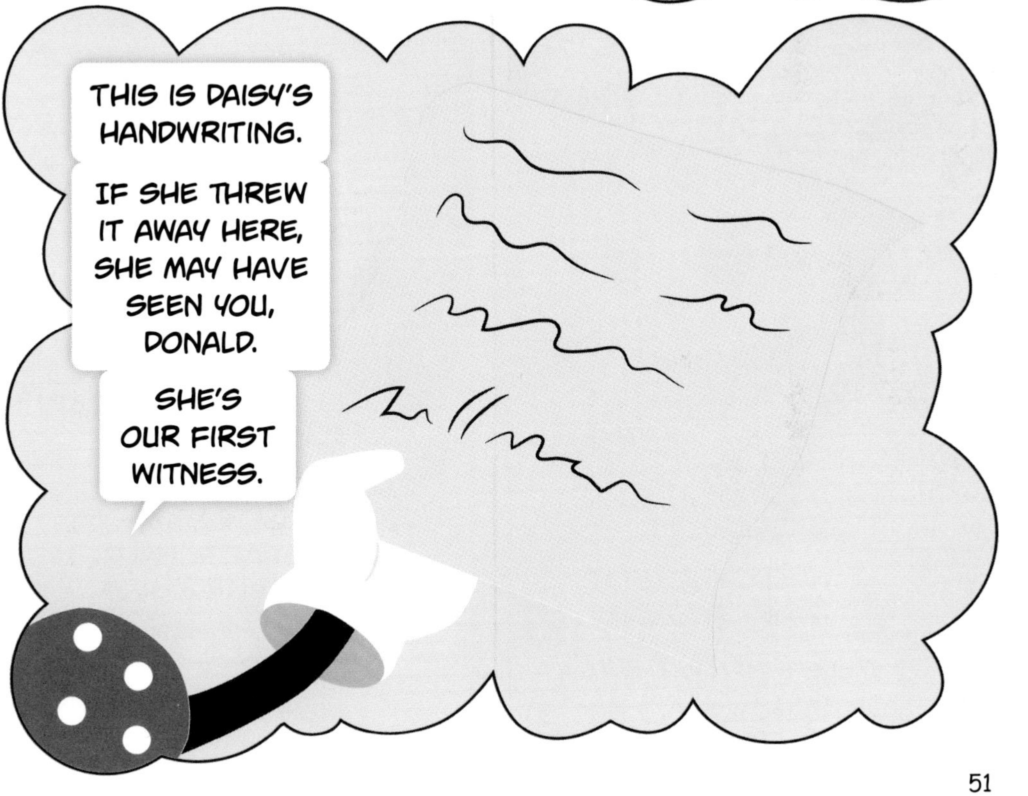
THIS IS DAISY'S HANDWRITING.
IF SHE THREW IT AWAY HERE, SHE MAY HAVE SEEN YOU, DONALD.
SHE'S OUR FIRST WITNESS.

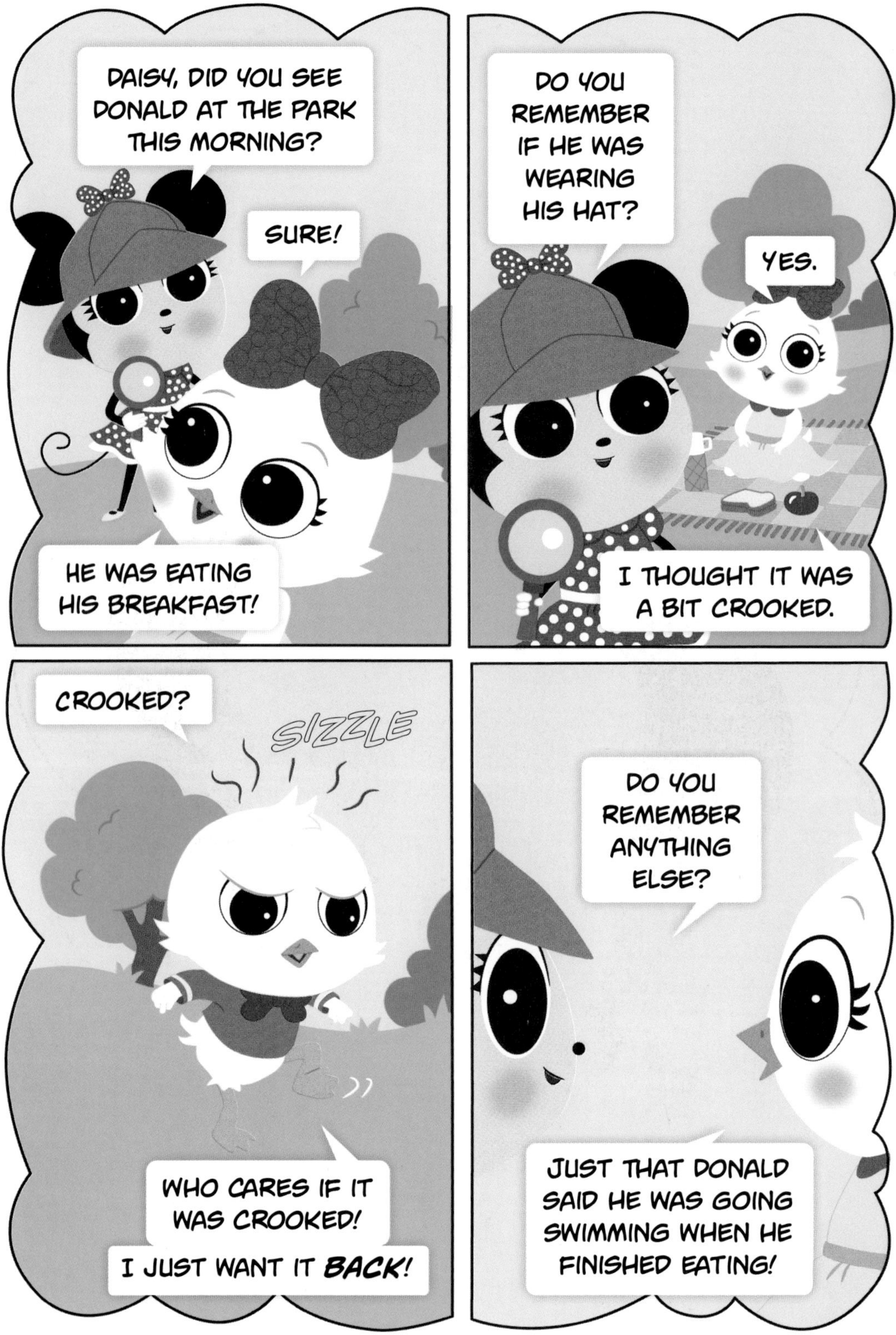
DAISY, DID YOU SEE DONALD AT THE PARK THIS MORNING?
SURE!
HE WAS EATING HIS BREAKFAST!
DO YOU REMEMBER IF HE WAS WEARING HIS HAT?
YES.
I THOUGHT IT WAS A BIT CROOKED.
CROOKED?
SIZZLE
WHO CARES IF IT WAS CROOKED!
I JUST WANT IT BACK!
DO YOU REMEMBER ANYTHING ELSE?
JUST THAT DONALD SAID HE WAS GOING SWIMMING WHEN HE FINISHED EATING!

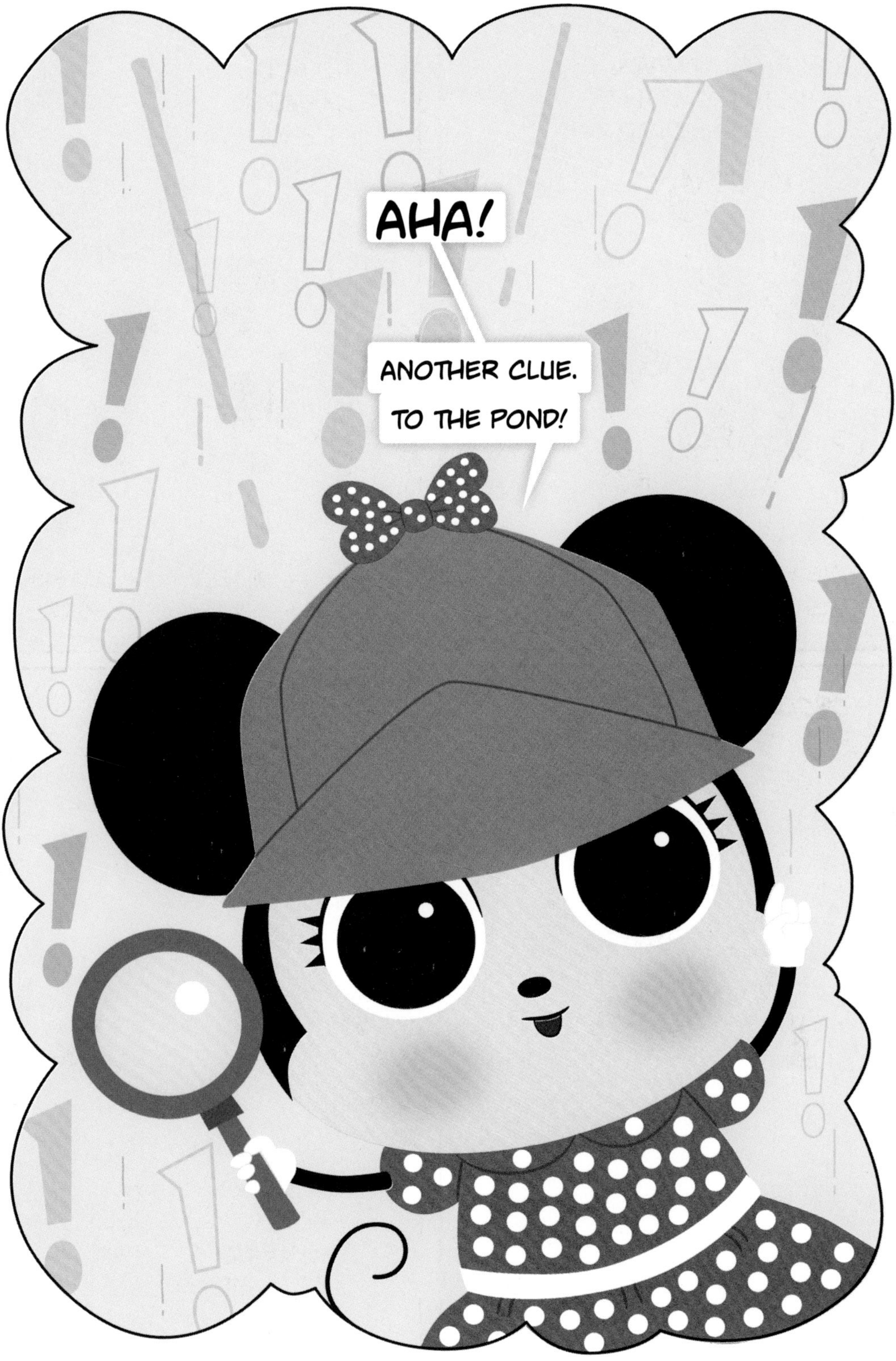
AHA!
ANOTHER CLUE.
TO THE POND!

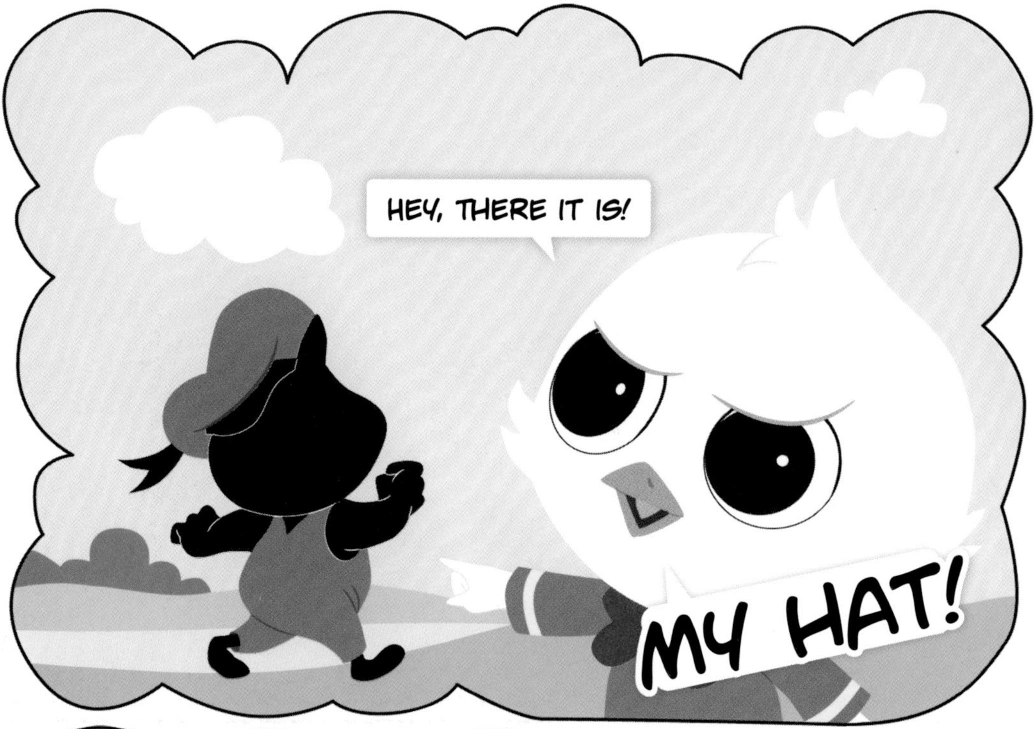
HEY, THERE IT IS!
MY HAT!

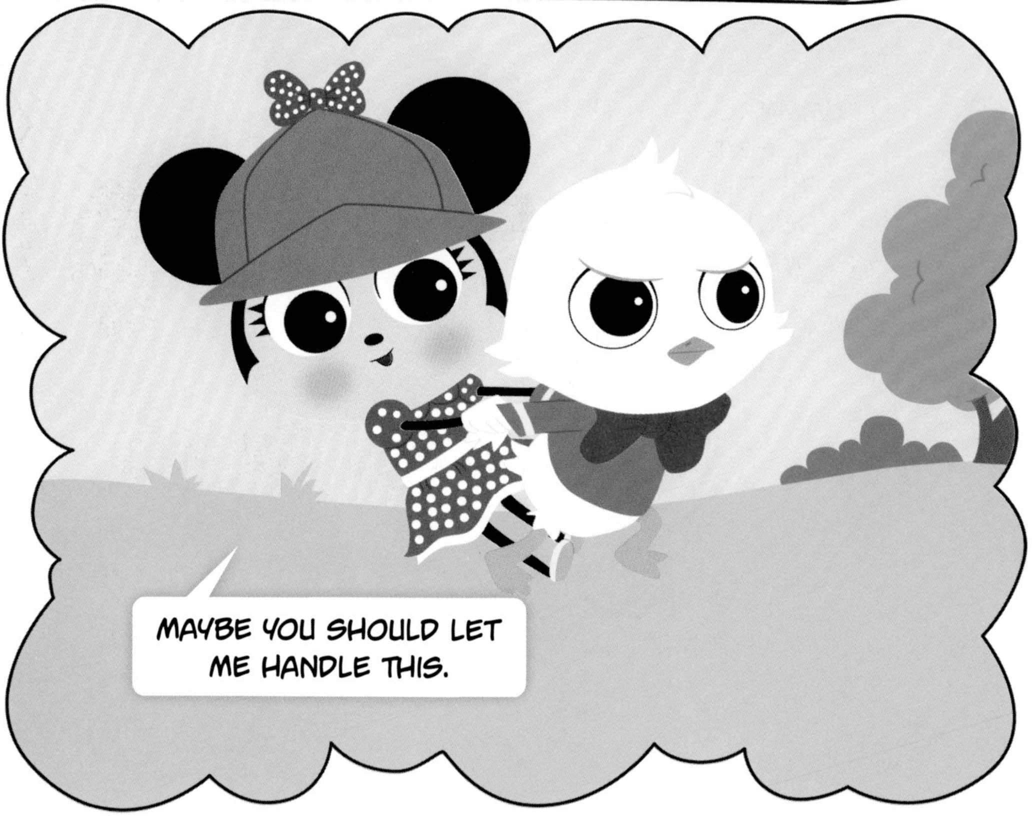
MAYBE YOU SHOULD LET ME HANDLE THIS.

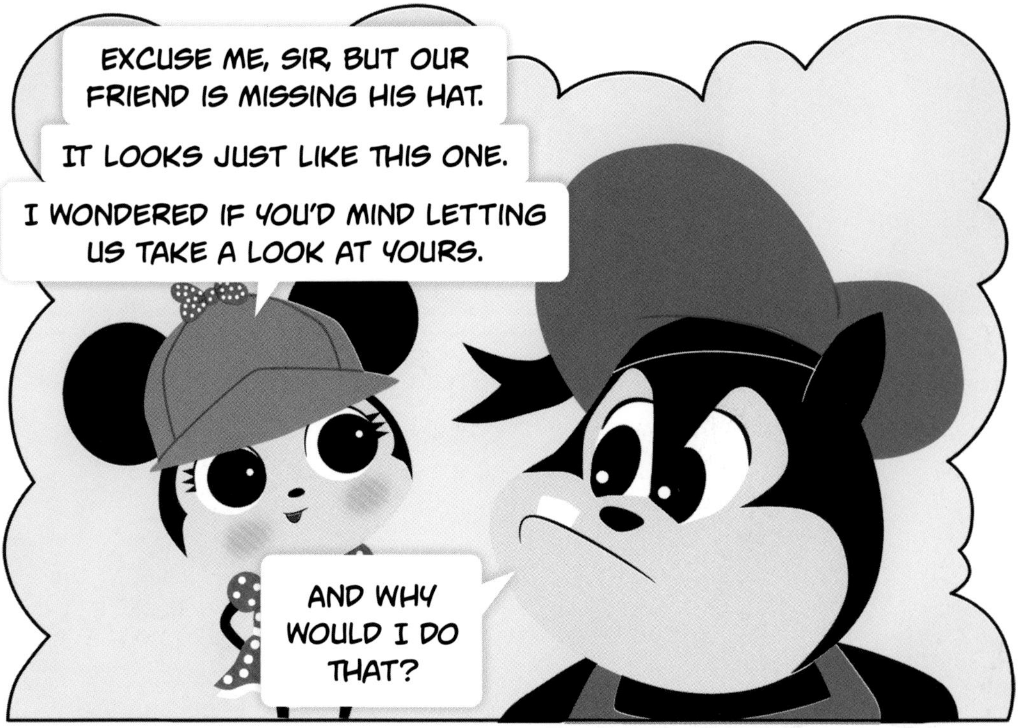
EXCUSE ME, SIR, BUT OUR FRIEND IS MISSING HIS HAT.
IT LOOKS JUST LIKE THIS ONE.
I WONDERED IF YOU'D MIND LETTING US TAKE A LOOK AT YOURS.
AND WHY WOULD I DO THAT?

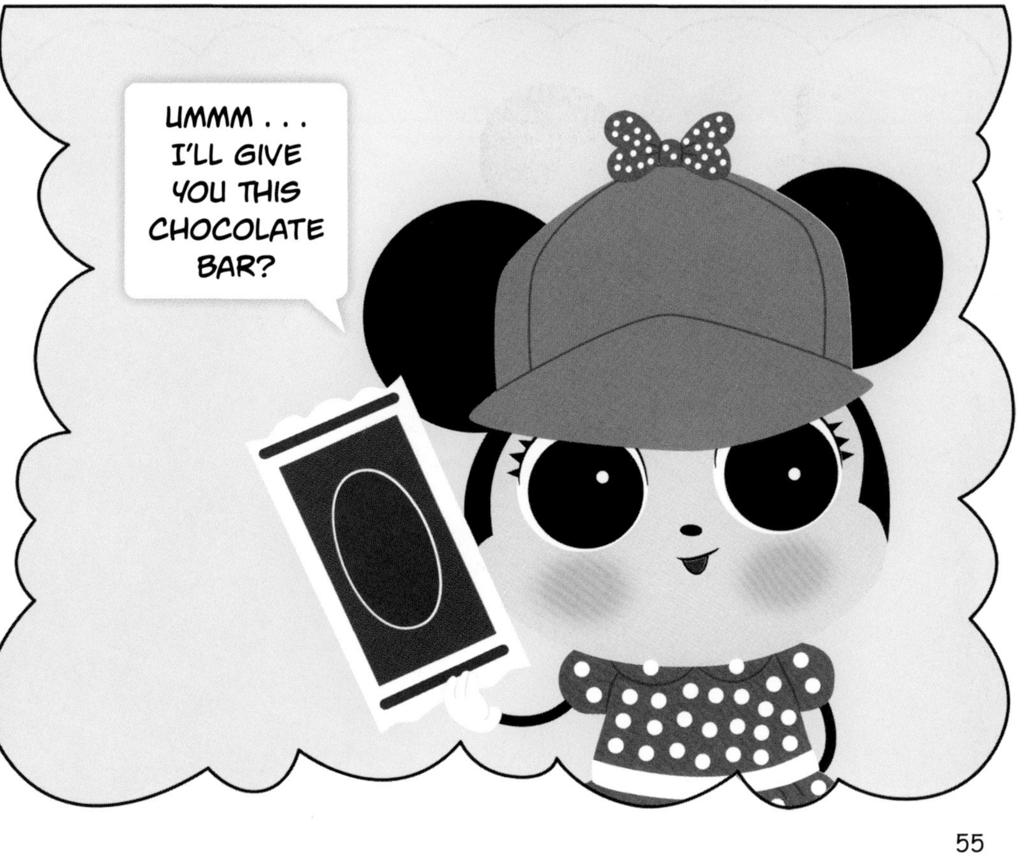
UMMM . . . I'LL GIVE YOU THIS CHOCOLATE BAR?

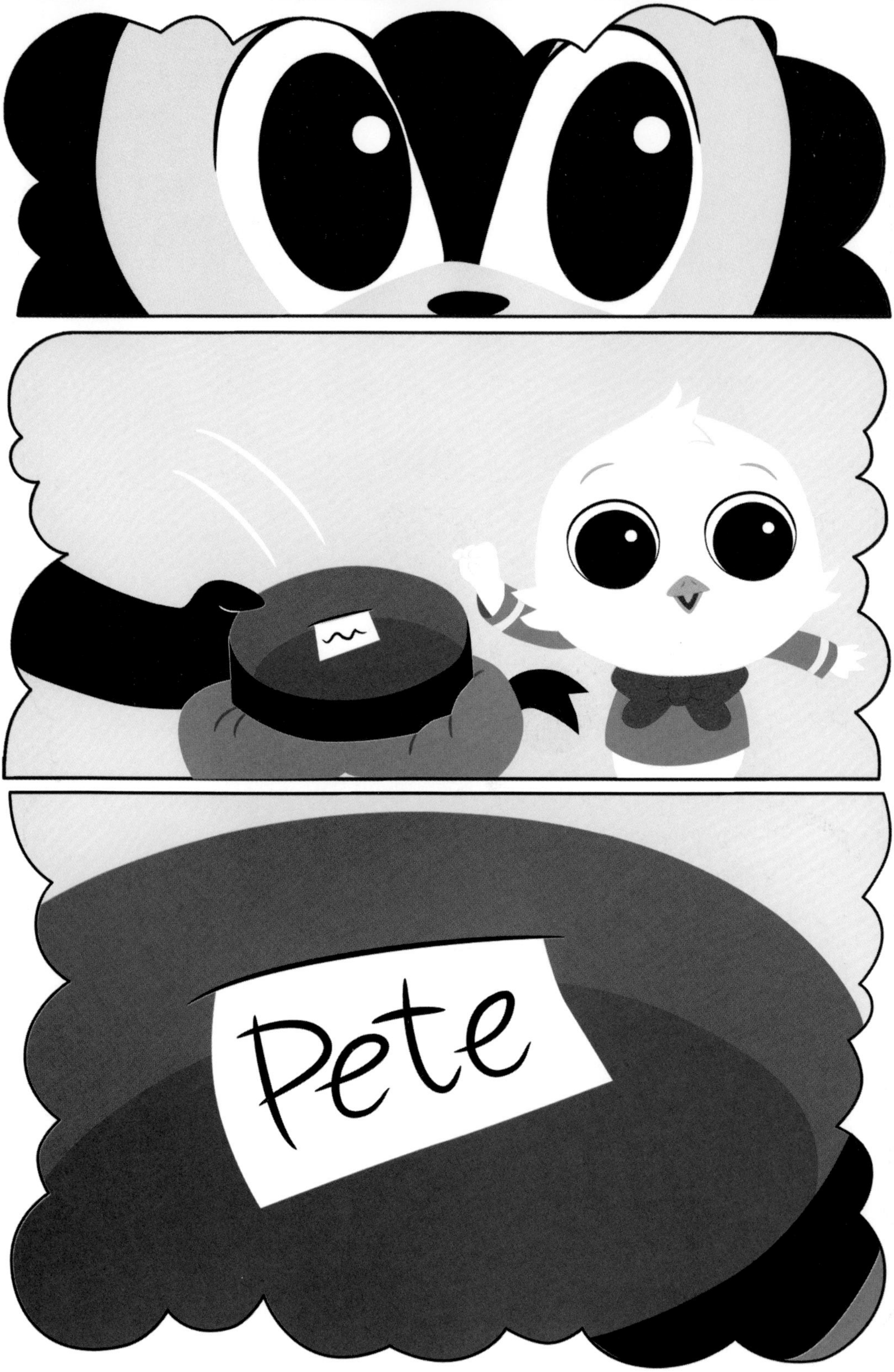
Pete

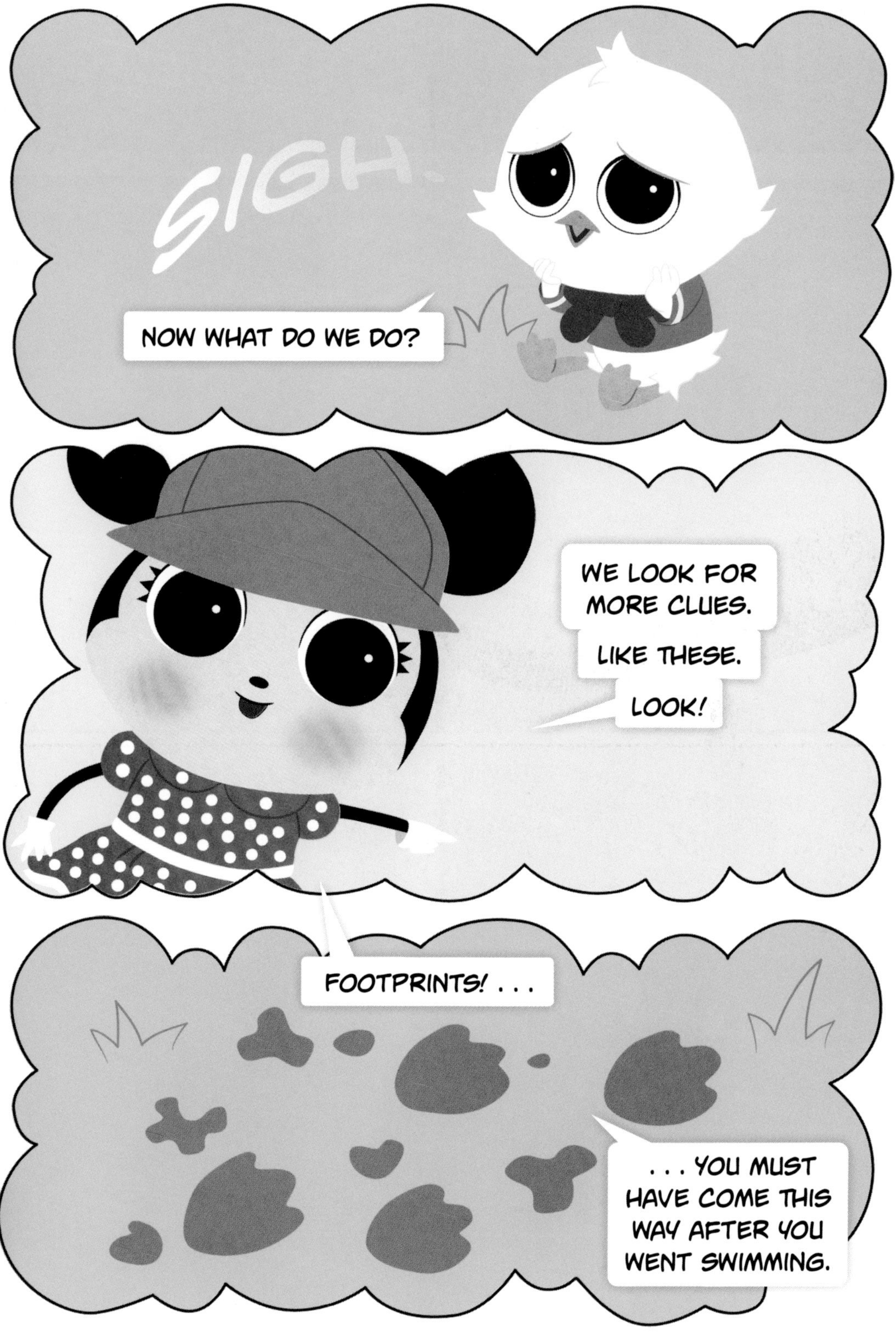
SIGH.
NOW WHAT DO WE DO?
WE LOOK FOR MORE CLUES.
LIKE THESE.
LOOK!
FOOTPRINTS! . . .
. . . YOU MUST HAVE COME THIS WAY AFTER YOU WENT SWIMMING.

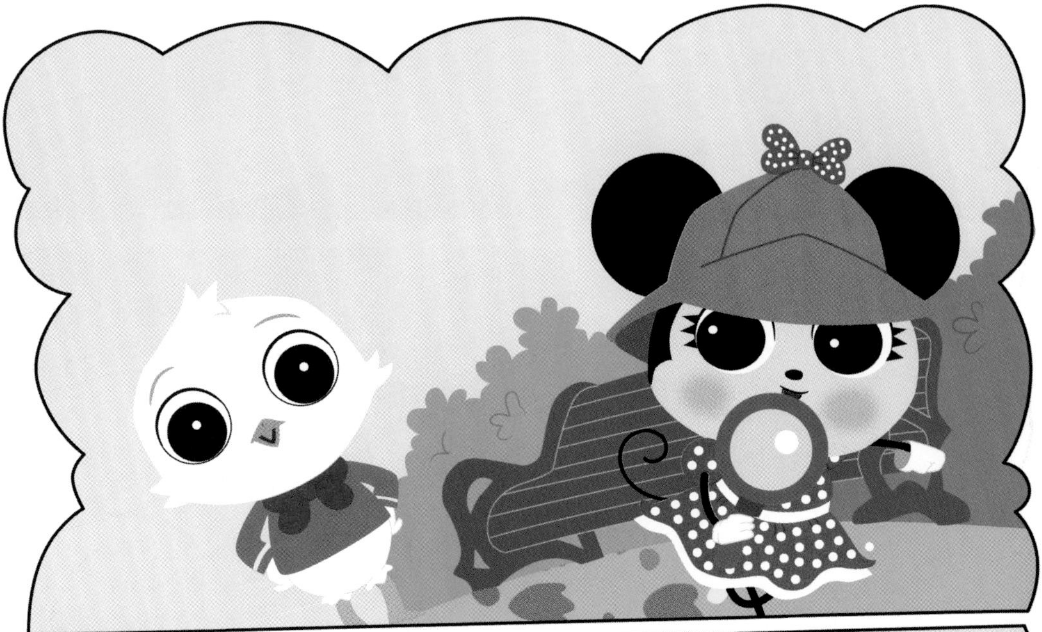

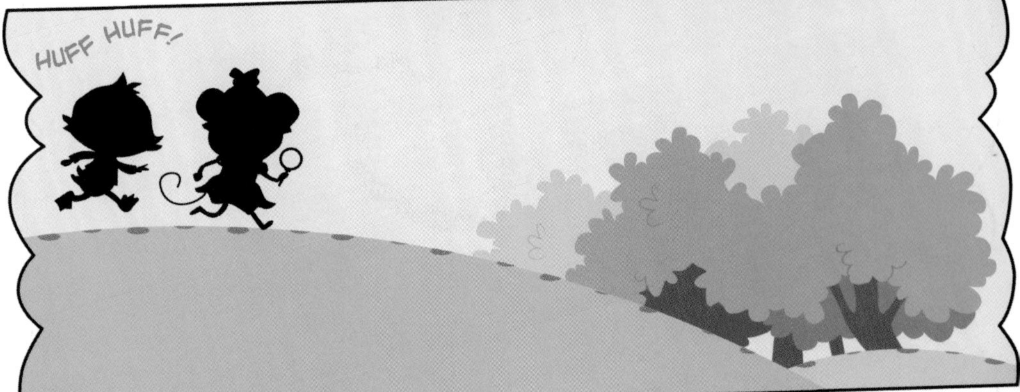
HUFF HUFF!

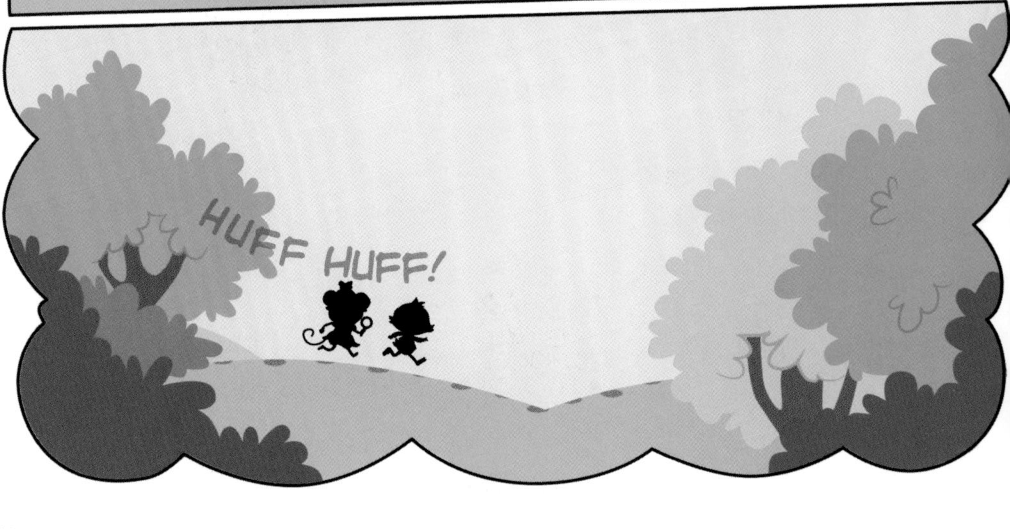
HUFF HUFF!

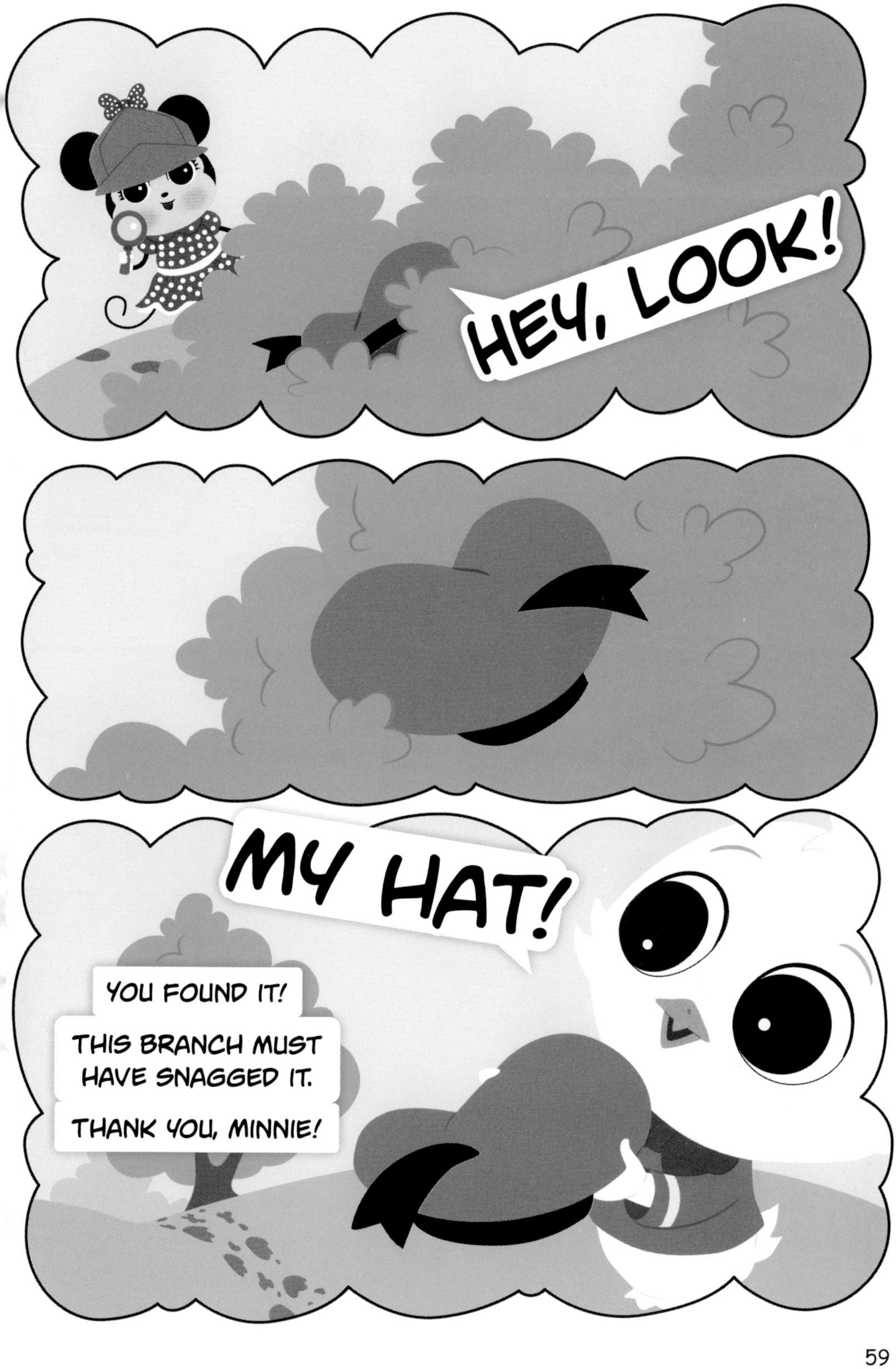
HEY, LOOK!
MY HAT!
YOU FOUND IT!
THIS BRANCH MUST HAVE SNAGGED IT.
THANK YOU, MINNIE!

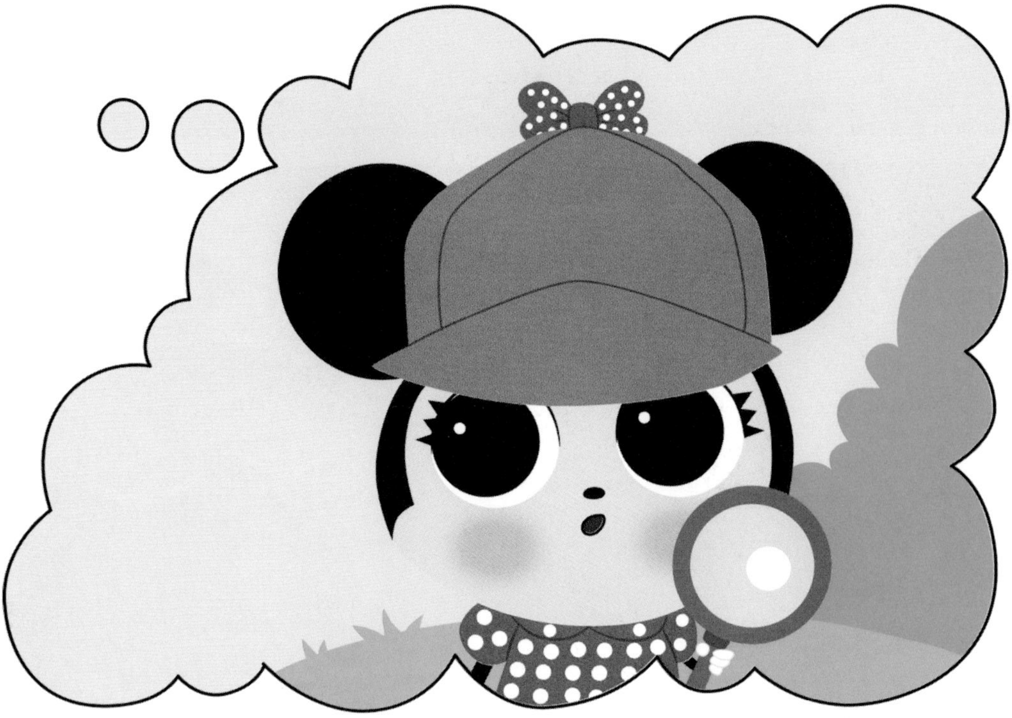

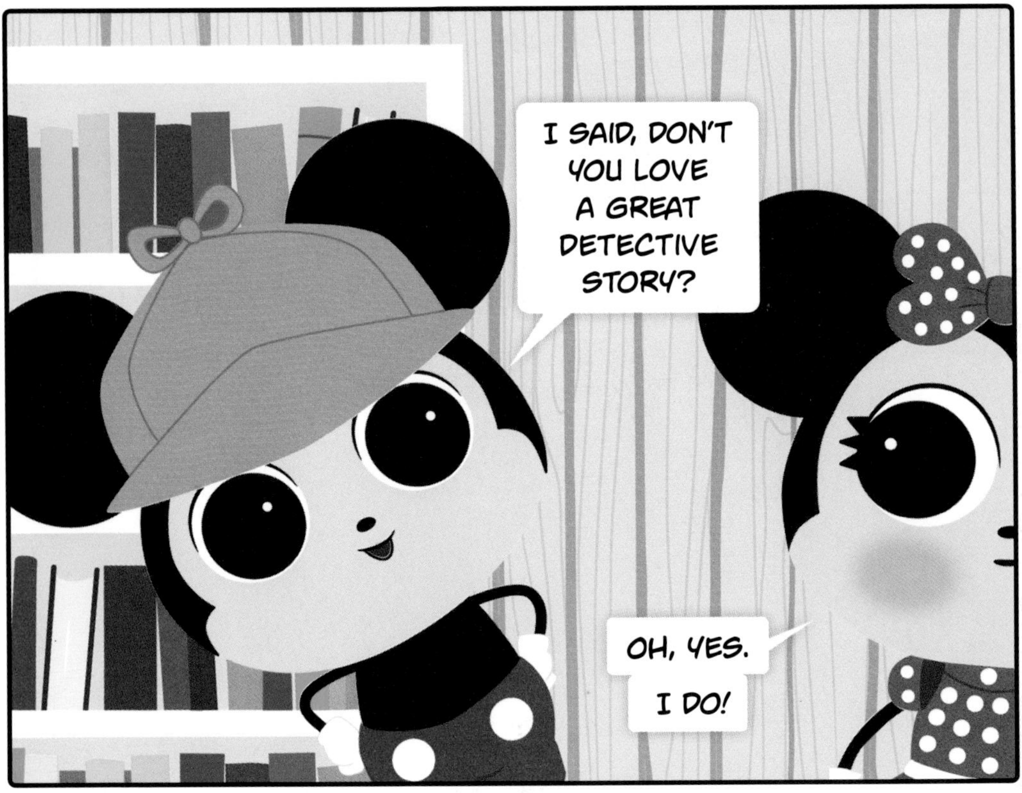
I SAID, DON'T YOU LOVE A GREAT DETECTIVE STORY?
OH, YES.
I DO!

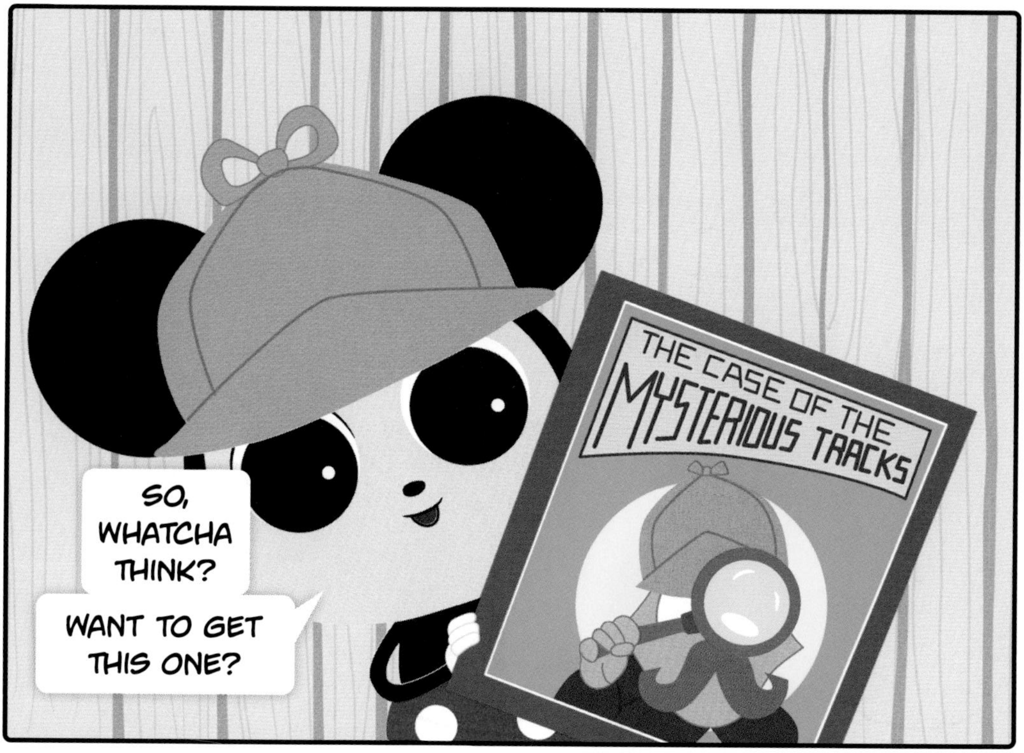
THE CASE OF THE MYSTERIOUS TRACKS
SO, WHATCHA THINK?
WANT TO GET THIS ONE?

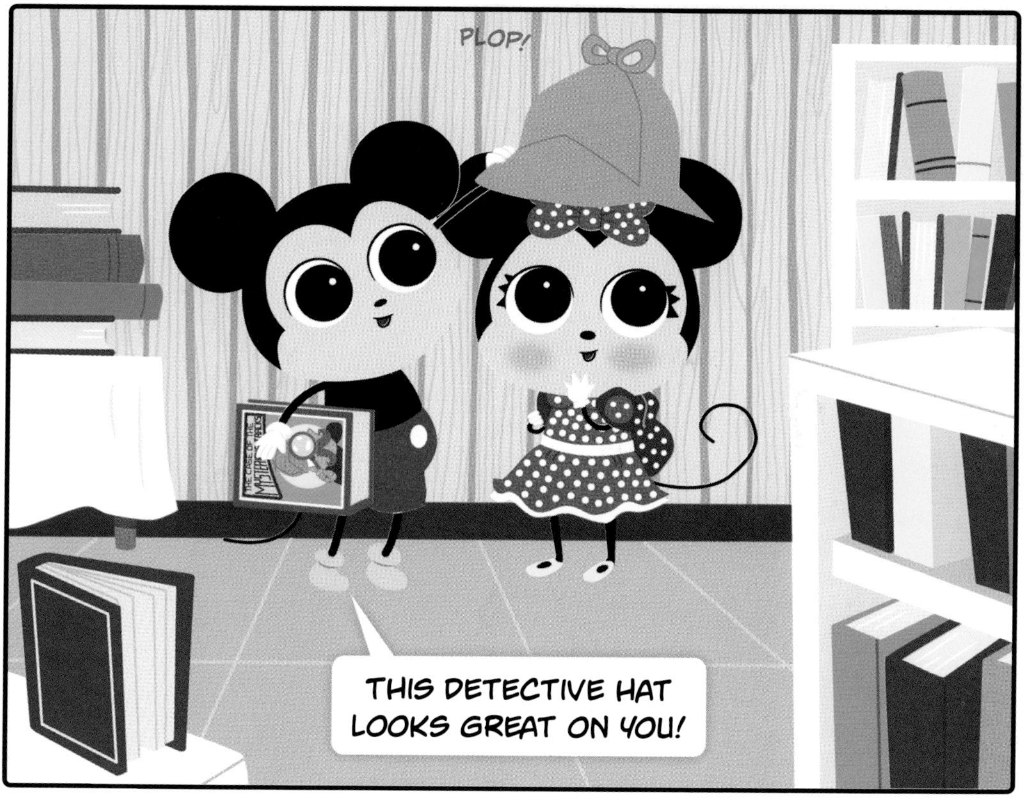
PLOP!
THIS DETECTIVE HAT LOOKS GREAT ON YOU!

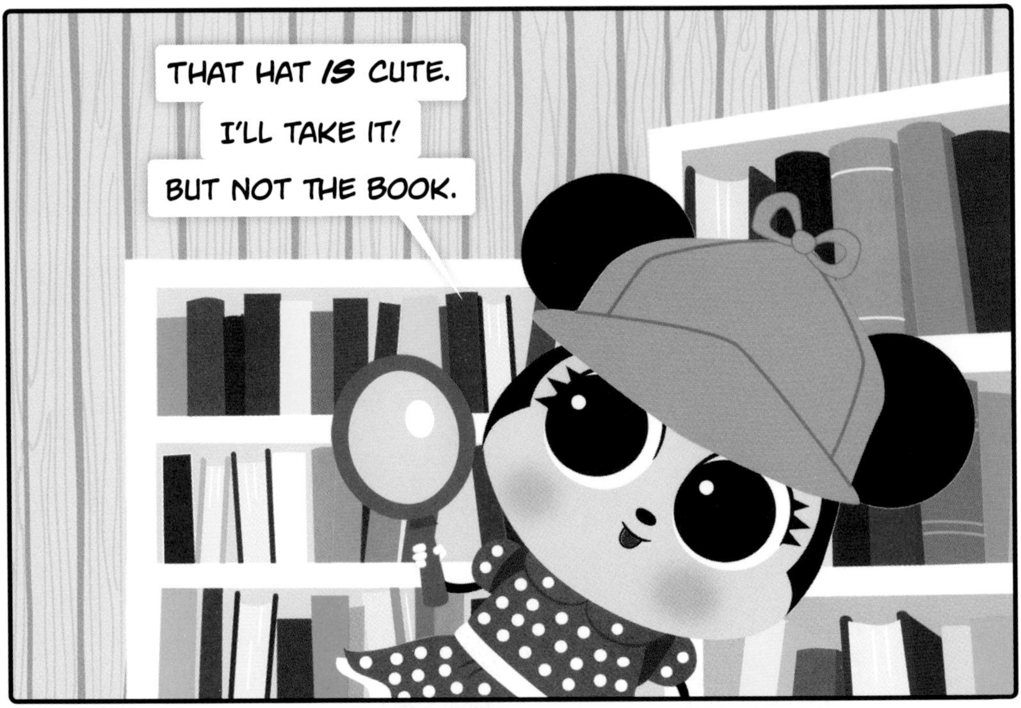
THAT HAT *IS* CUTE.
I'LL TAKE IT!
BUT NOT THE BOOK.

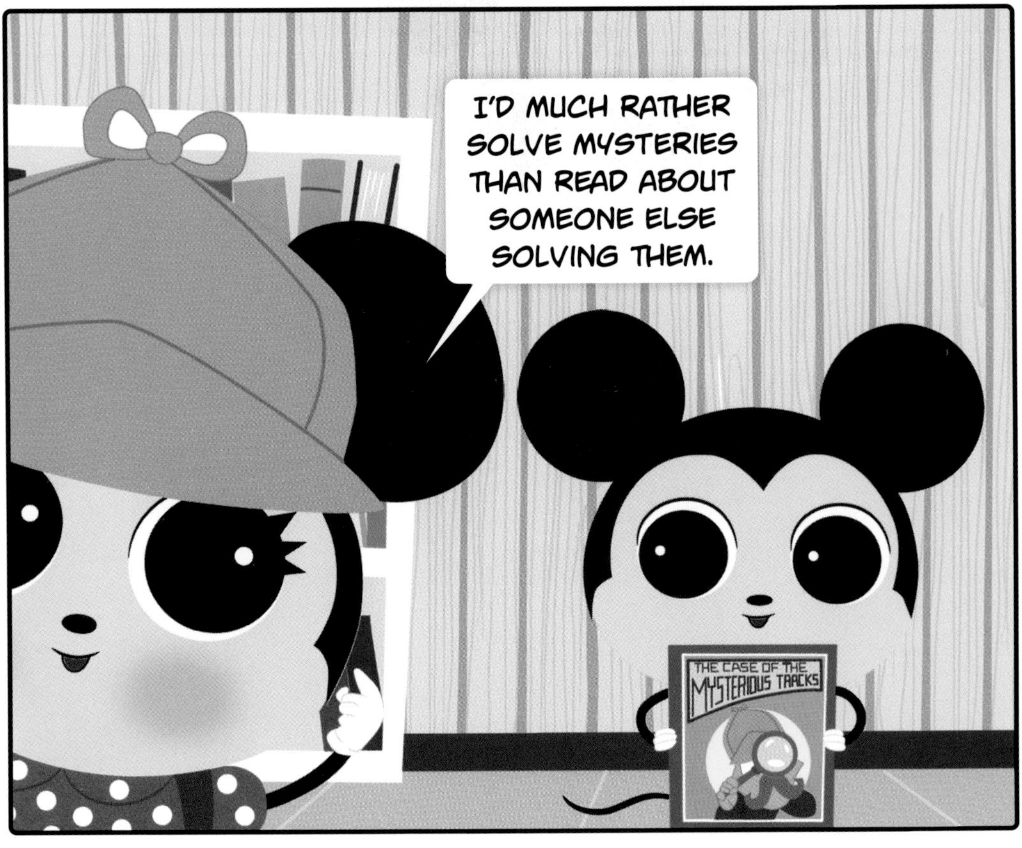
I'D MUCH RATHER SOLVE MYSTERIES THAN READ ABOUT SOMEONE ELSE SOLVING THEM.
THE CASE OF THE MYSTERIOUS TRACKS

PART 4

THE PERFECT BOOK?

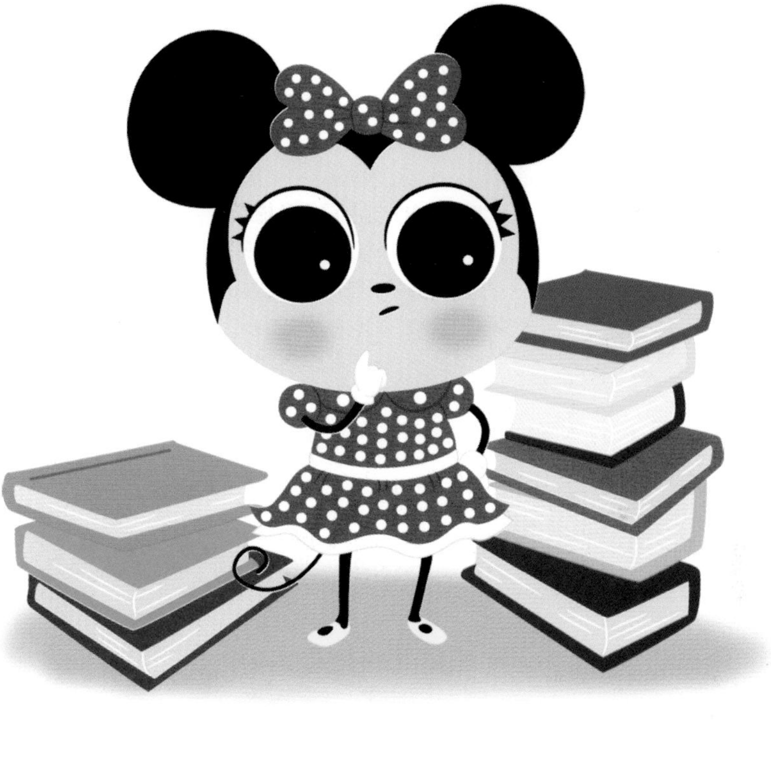

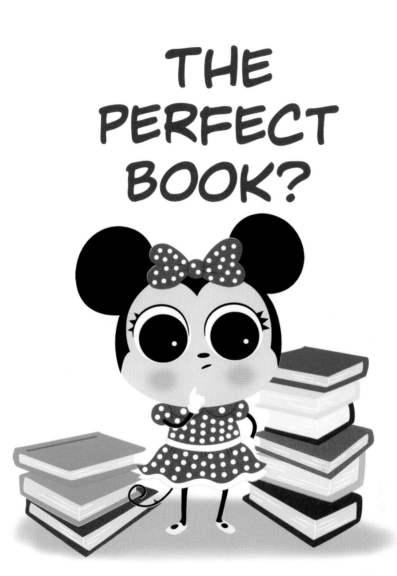

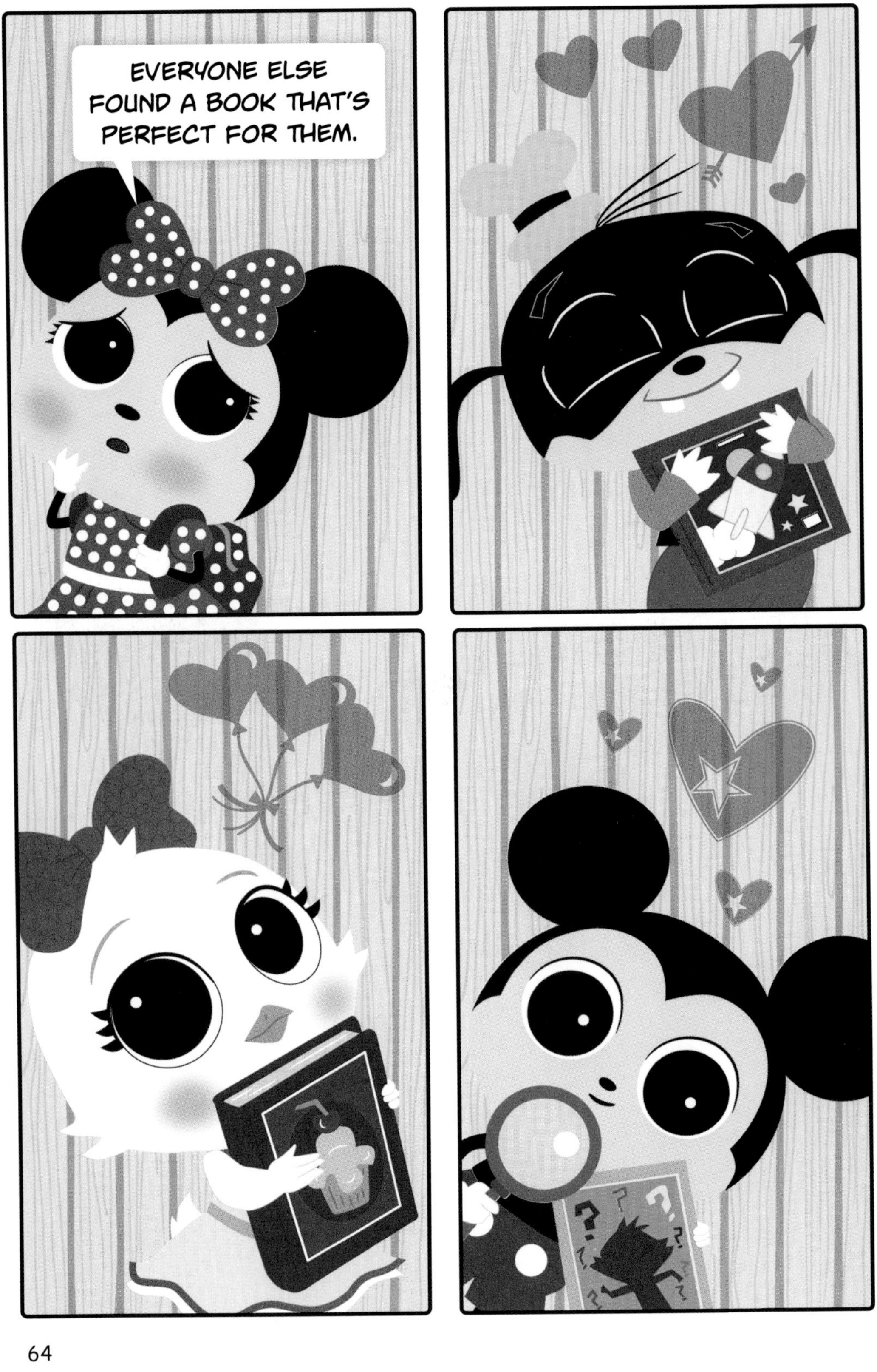
EVERYONE ELSE FOUND A BOOK THAT'S PERFECT FOR THEM.

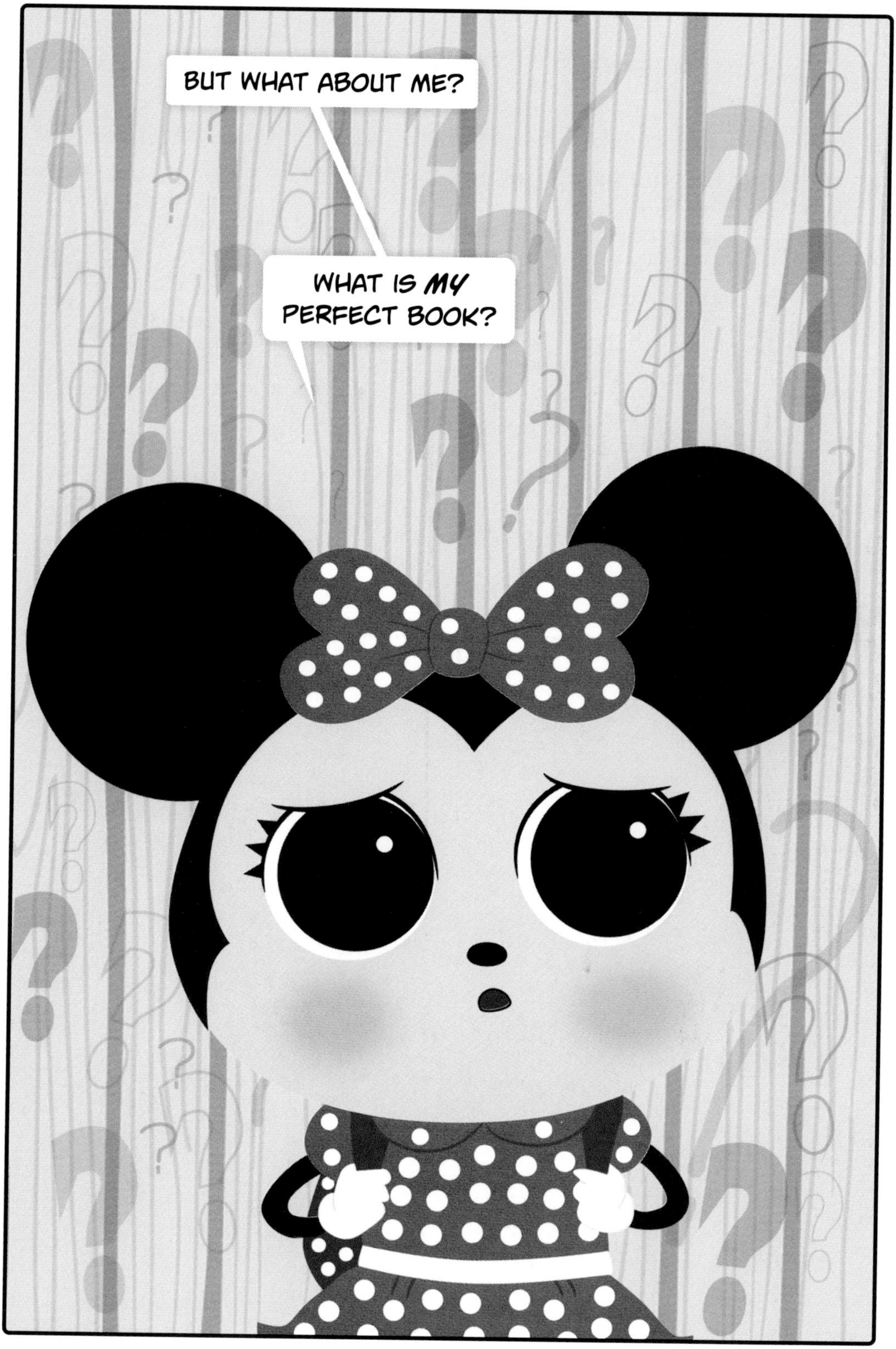
BUT WHAT ABOUT ME?
WHAT IS *MY* PERFECT BOOK?

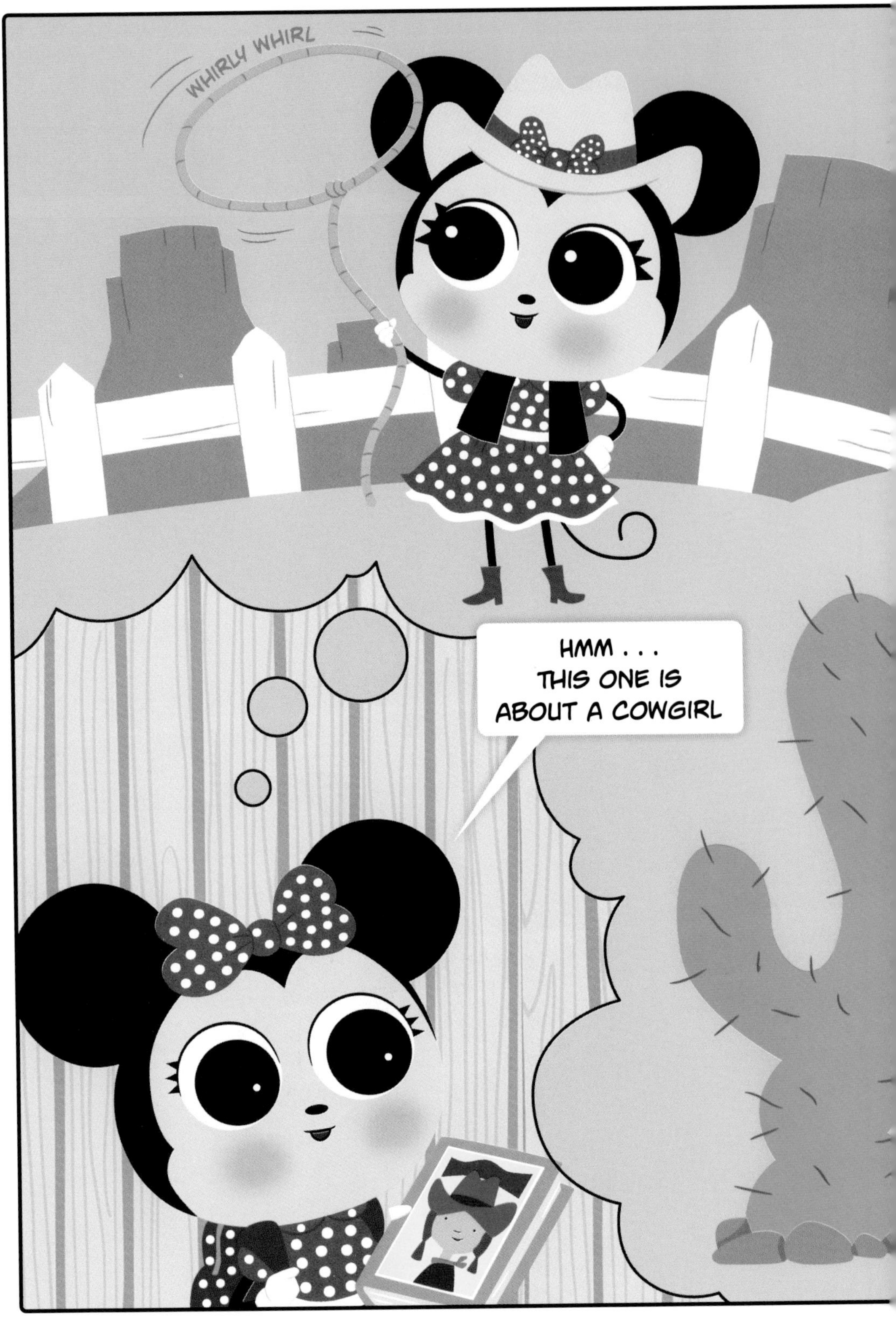
WHIRLY WHIRL
HMM . . . THIS ONE IS ABOUT A COWGIRL

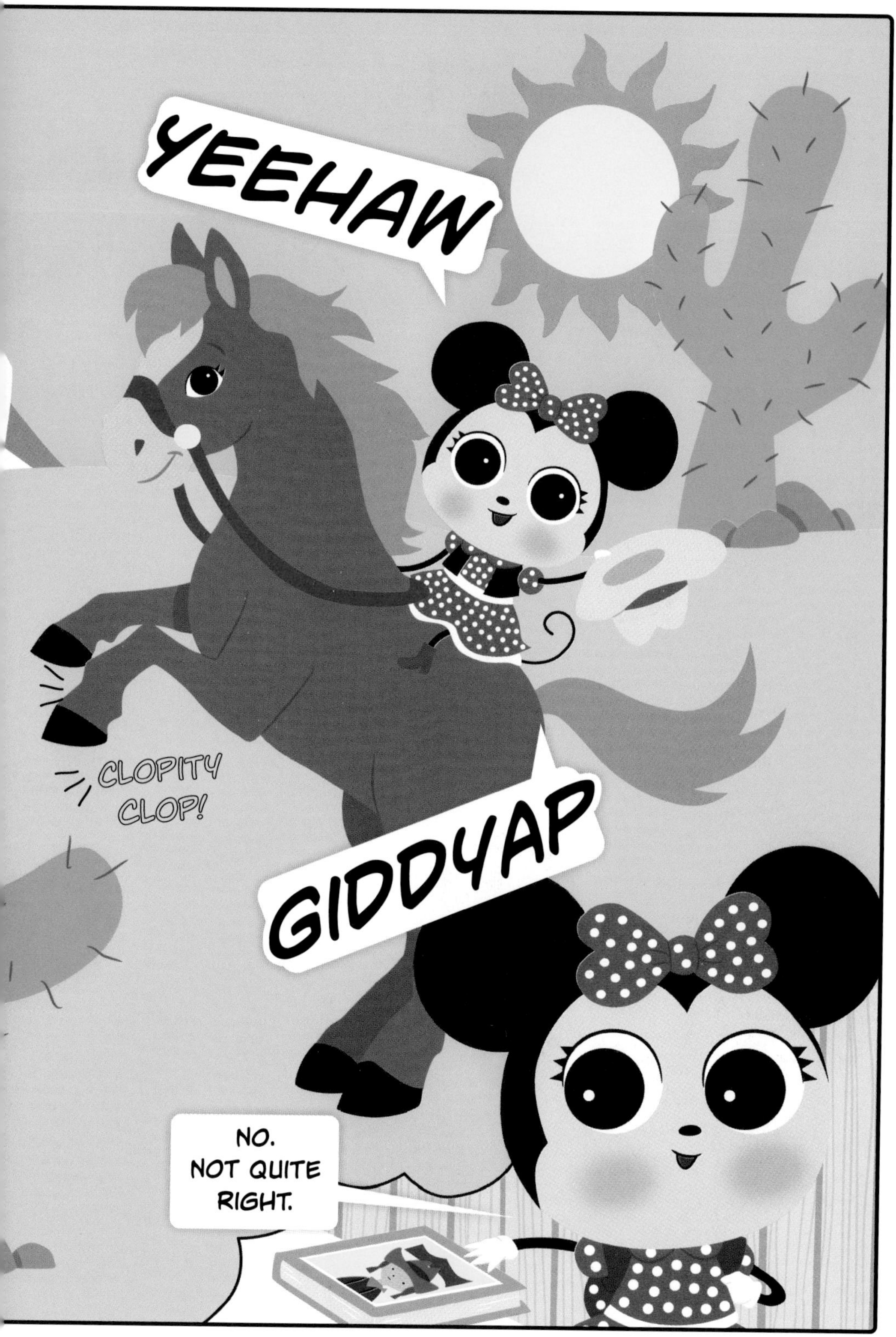
YEEHAW
CLOPITY CLOP!
GIDDYAP
NO. NOT QUITE RIGHT.

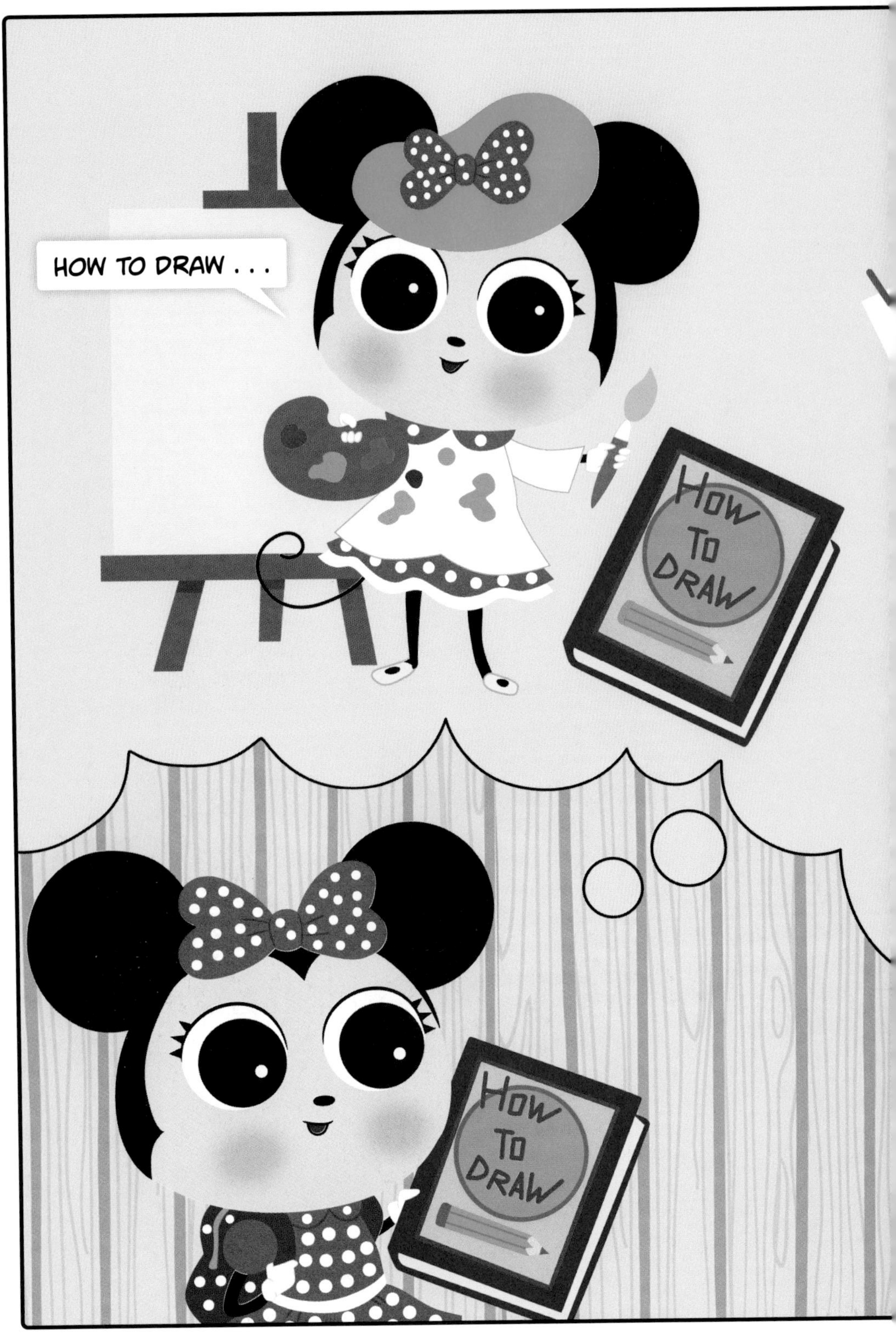
HOW TO DRAW . . .
How To Draw
How To Draw

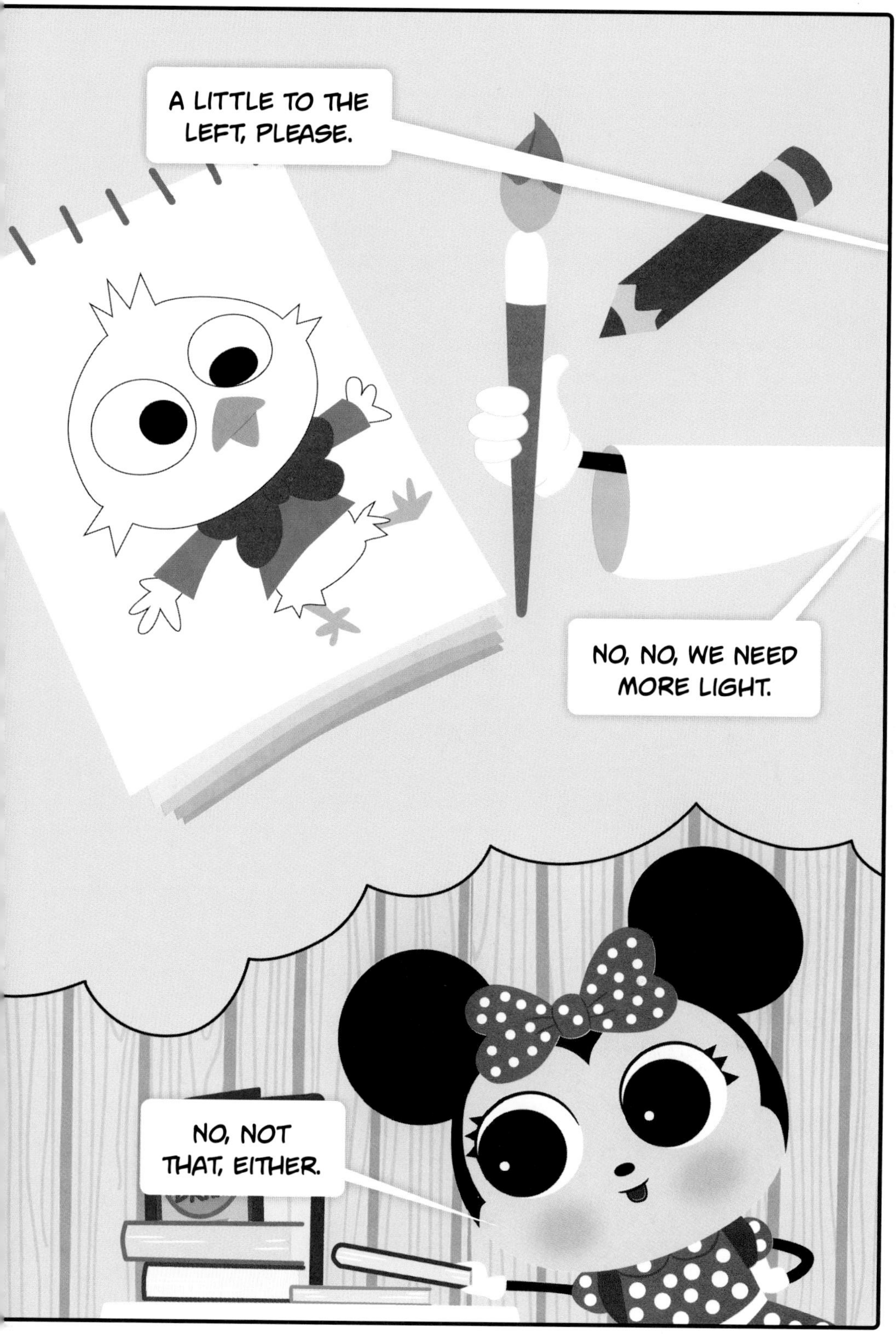
A LITTLE TO THE LEFT, PLEASE.
NO, NO, WE NEED MORE LIGHT.
NO, NOT THAT, EITHER.

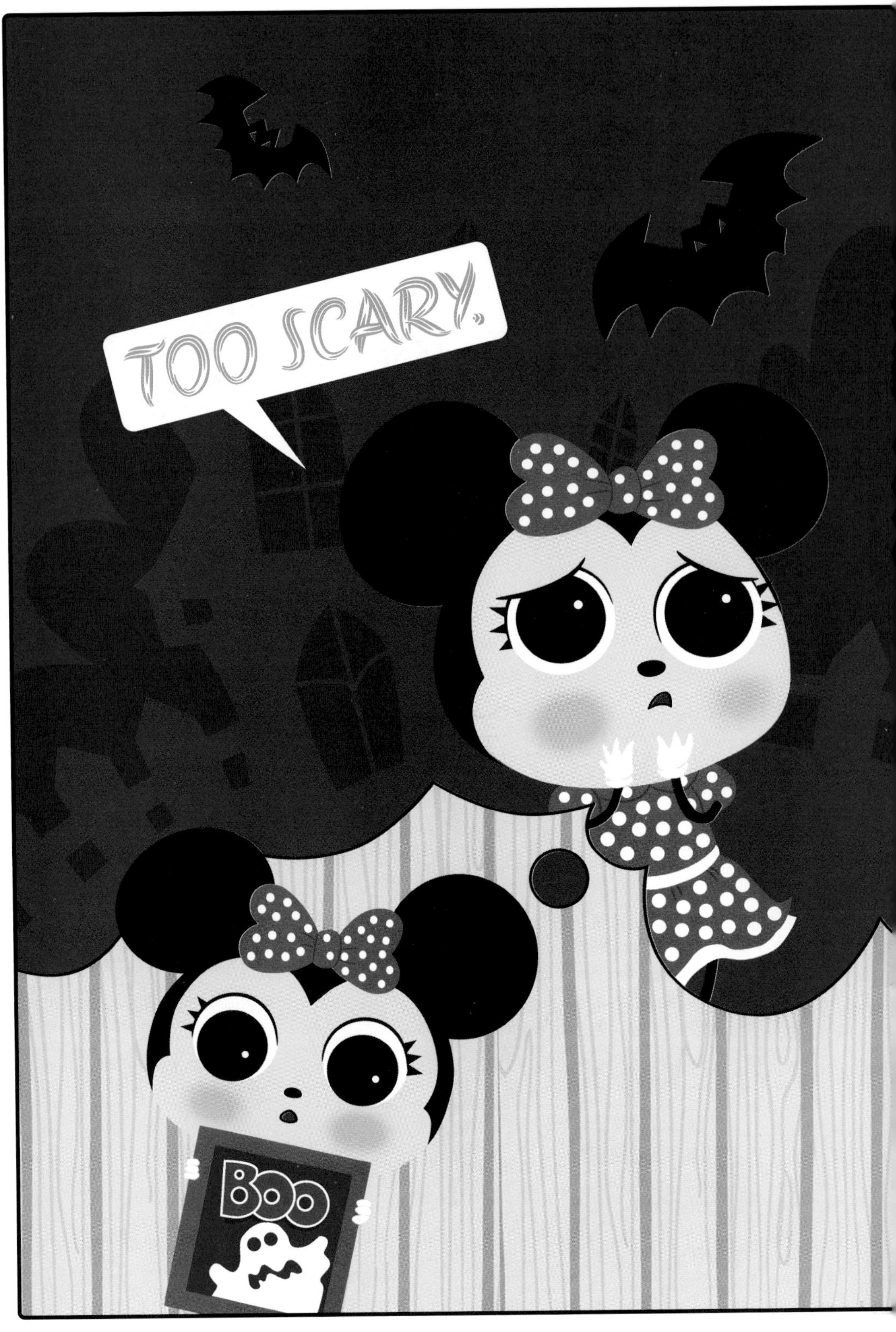
TOO SCARY.
BOO

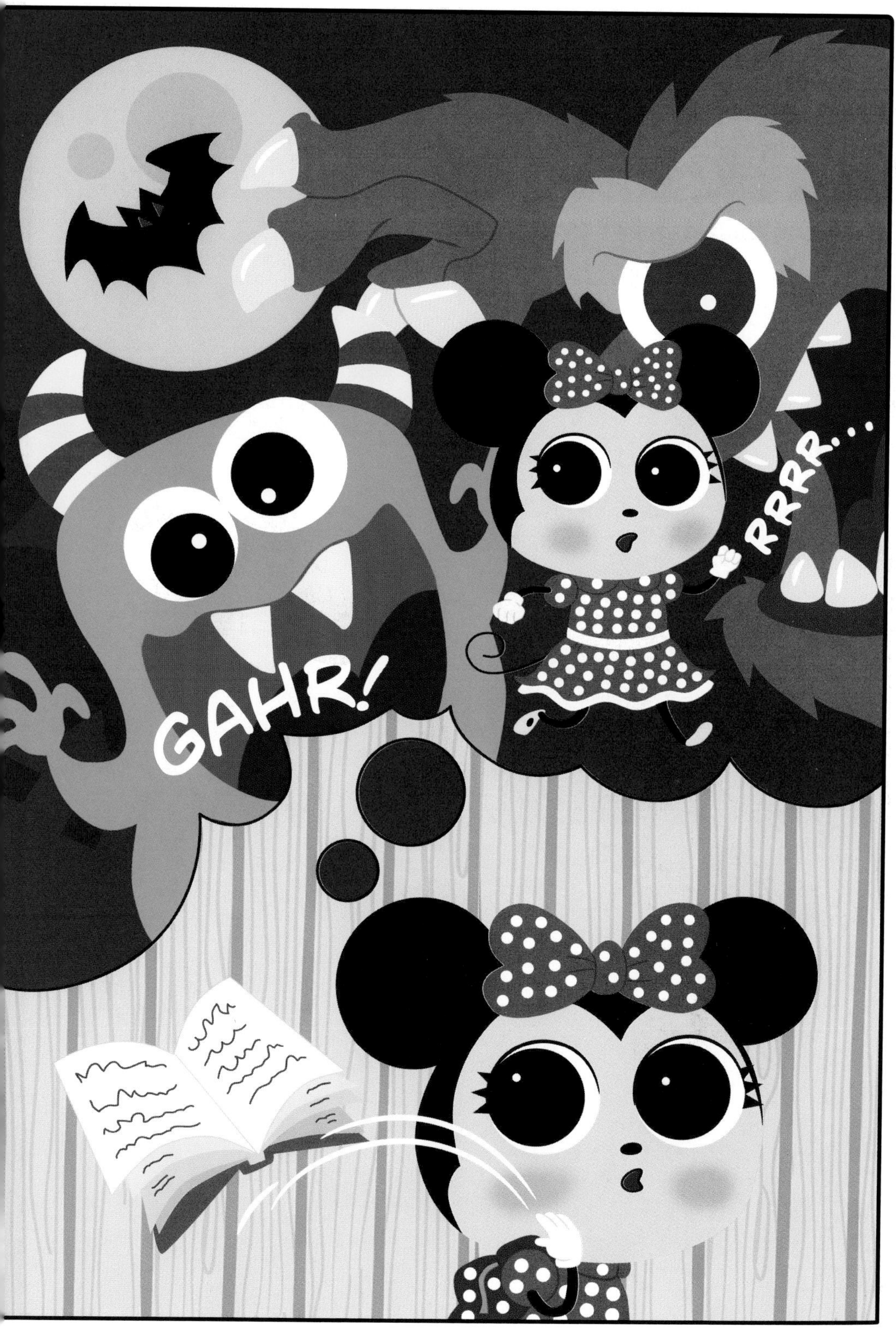
GAHR!
RRRR…

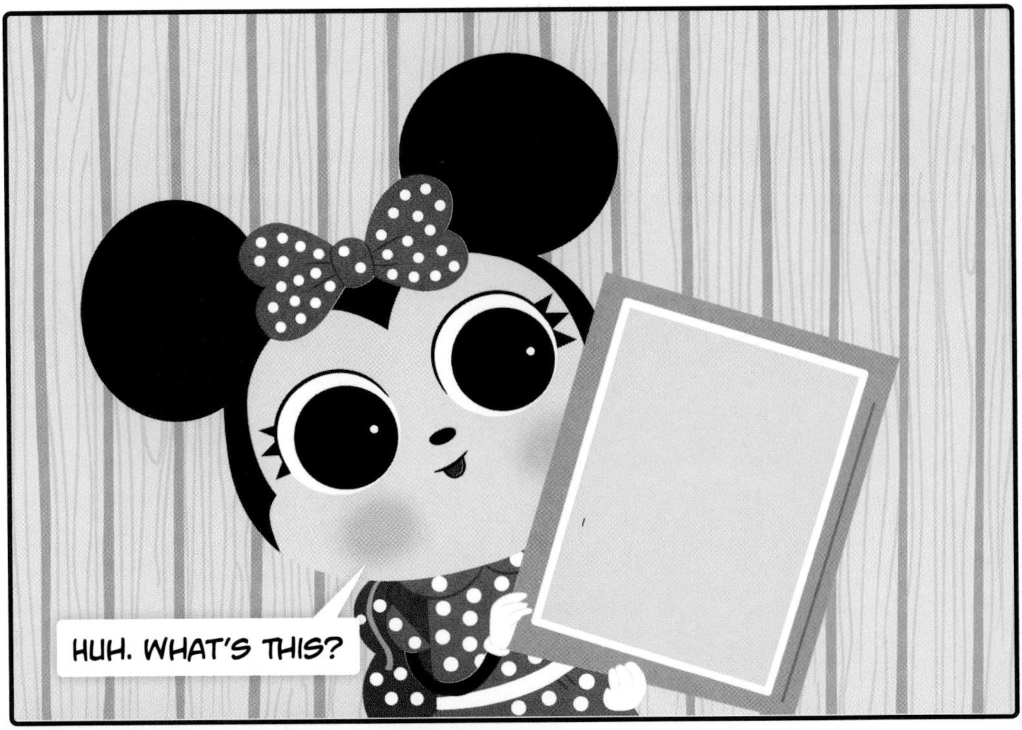
HUH. WHAT'S THIS?

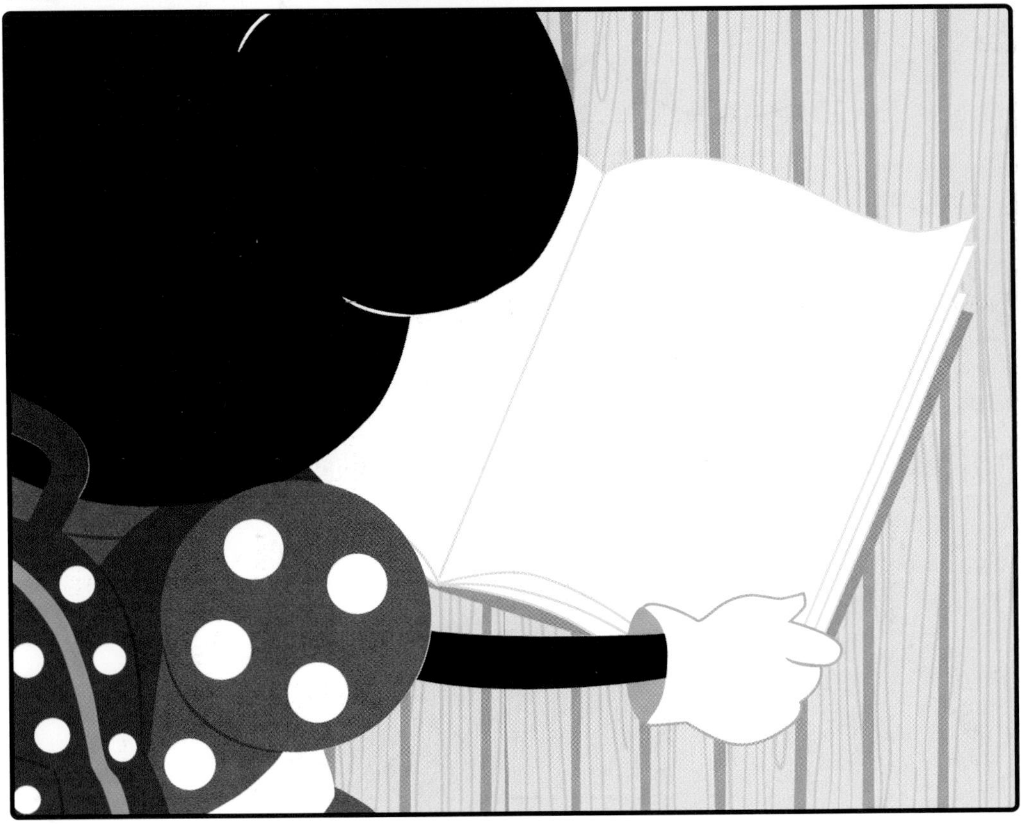

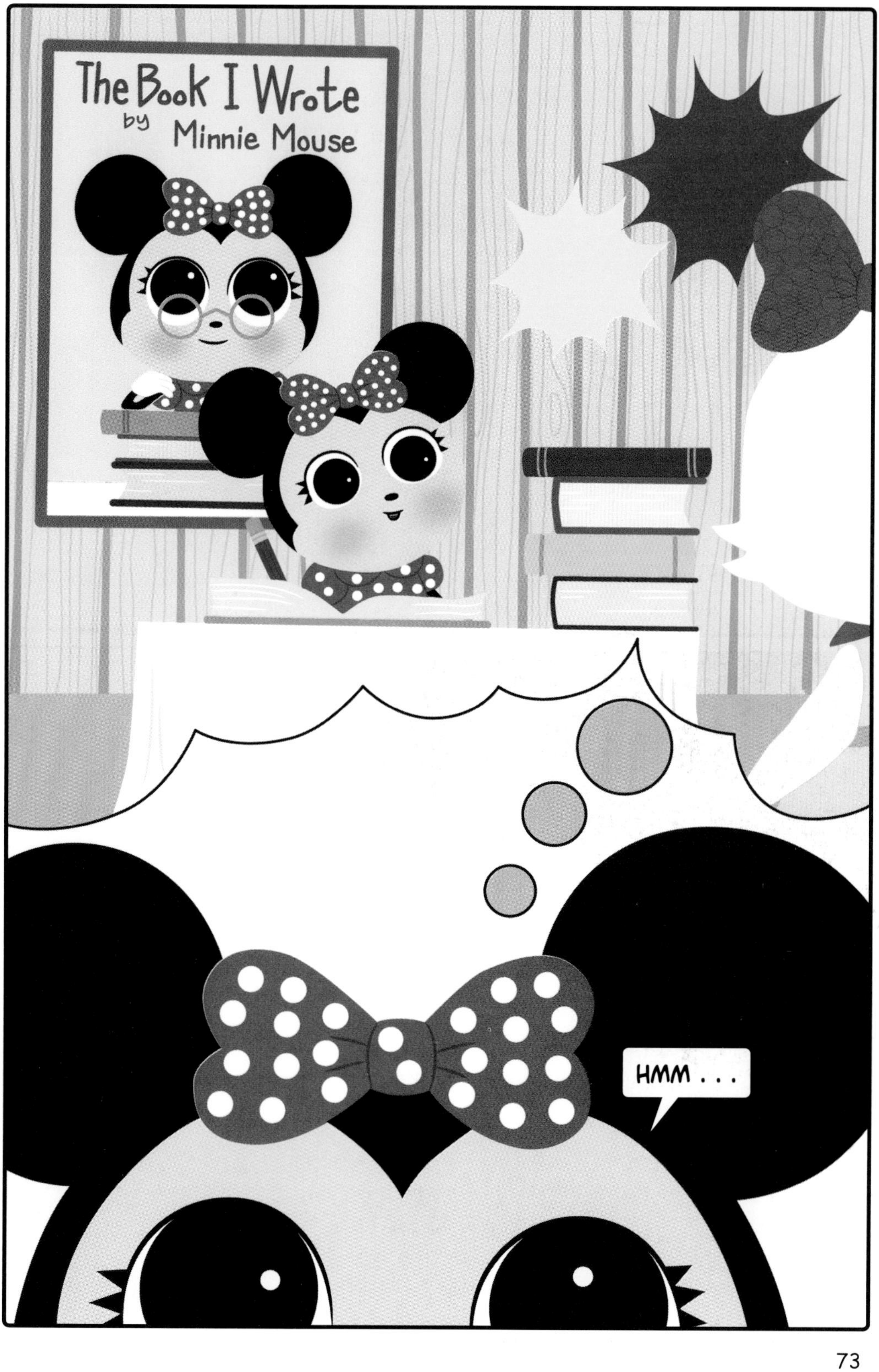
The Book I Wrote
by Minnie Mouse
HMM . . .

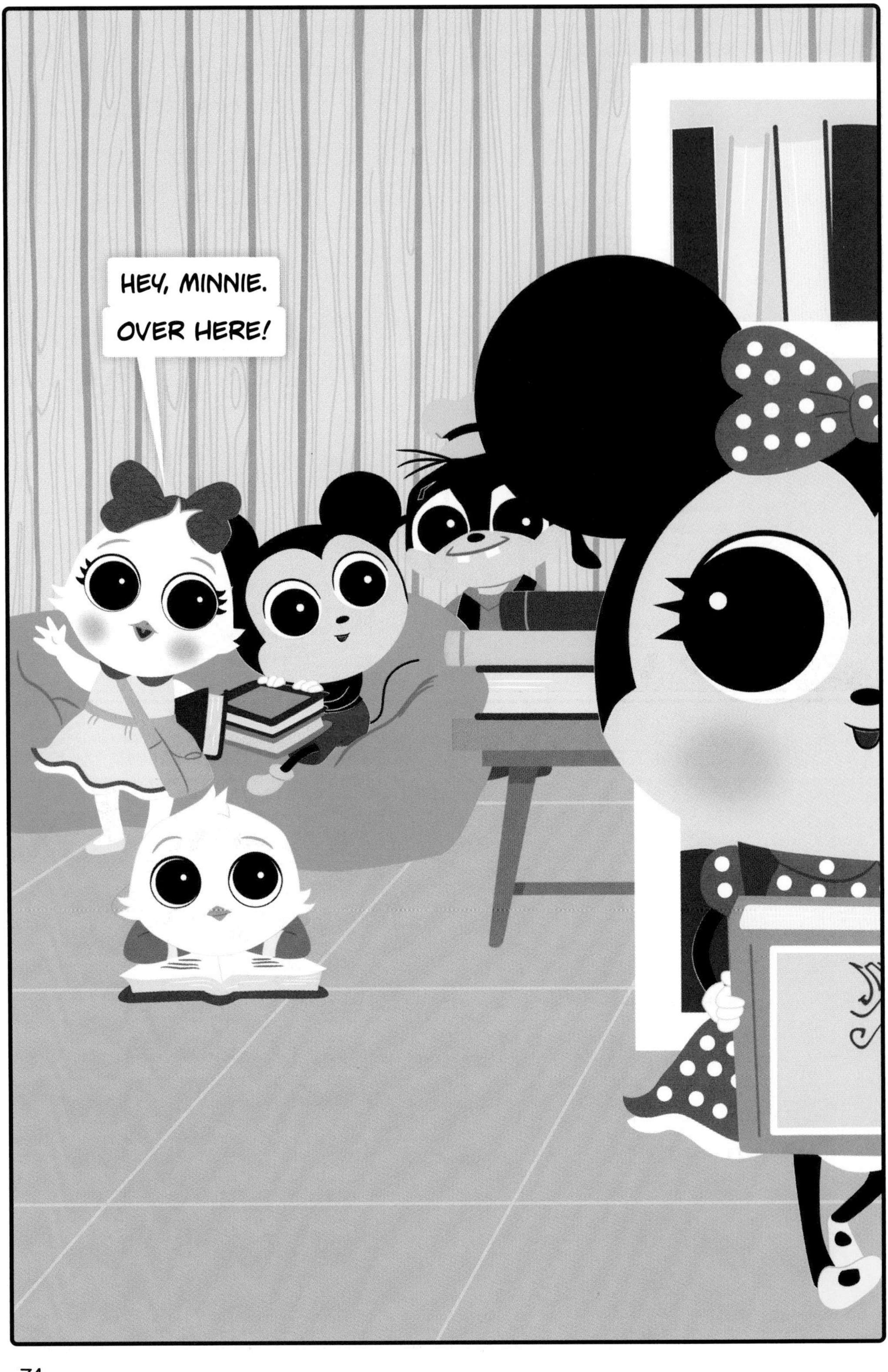
HEY, MINNIE. OVER HERE!

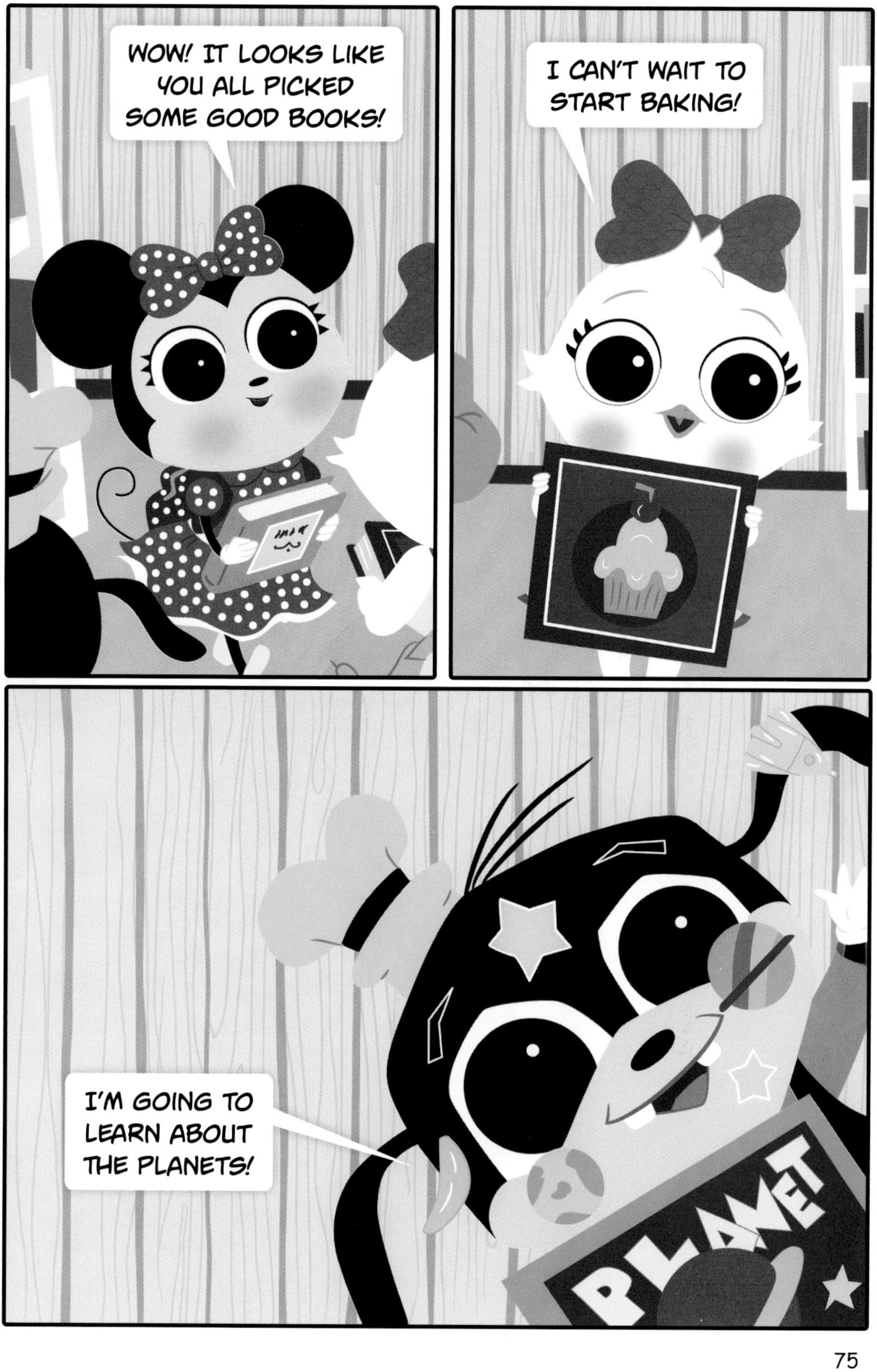
WOW! IT LOOKS LIKE YOU ALL PICKED SOME GOOD BOOKS!
I CAN'T WAIT TO START BAKING!
I'M GOING TO LEARN ABOUT THE PLANETS!
PLANET

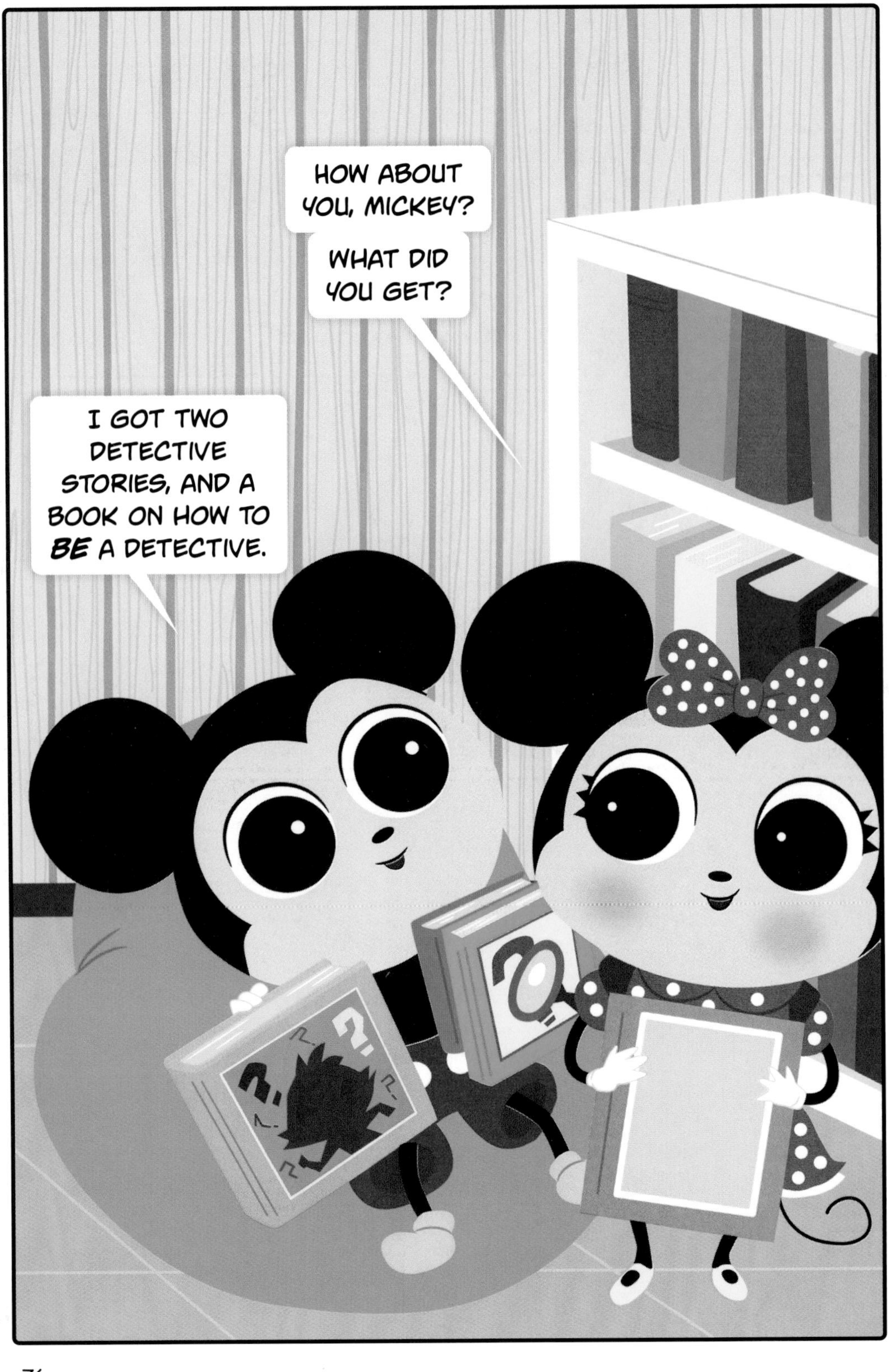
HOW ABOUT YOU, MICKEY?
WHAT DID YOU GET?
I GOT TWO DETECTIVE STORIES, AND A BOOK ON HOW TO *BE* A DETECTIVE.

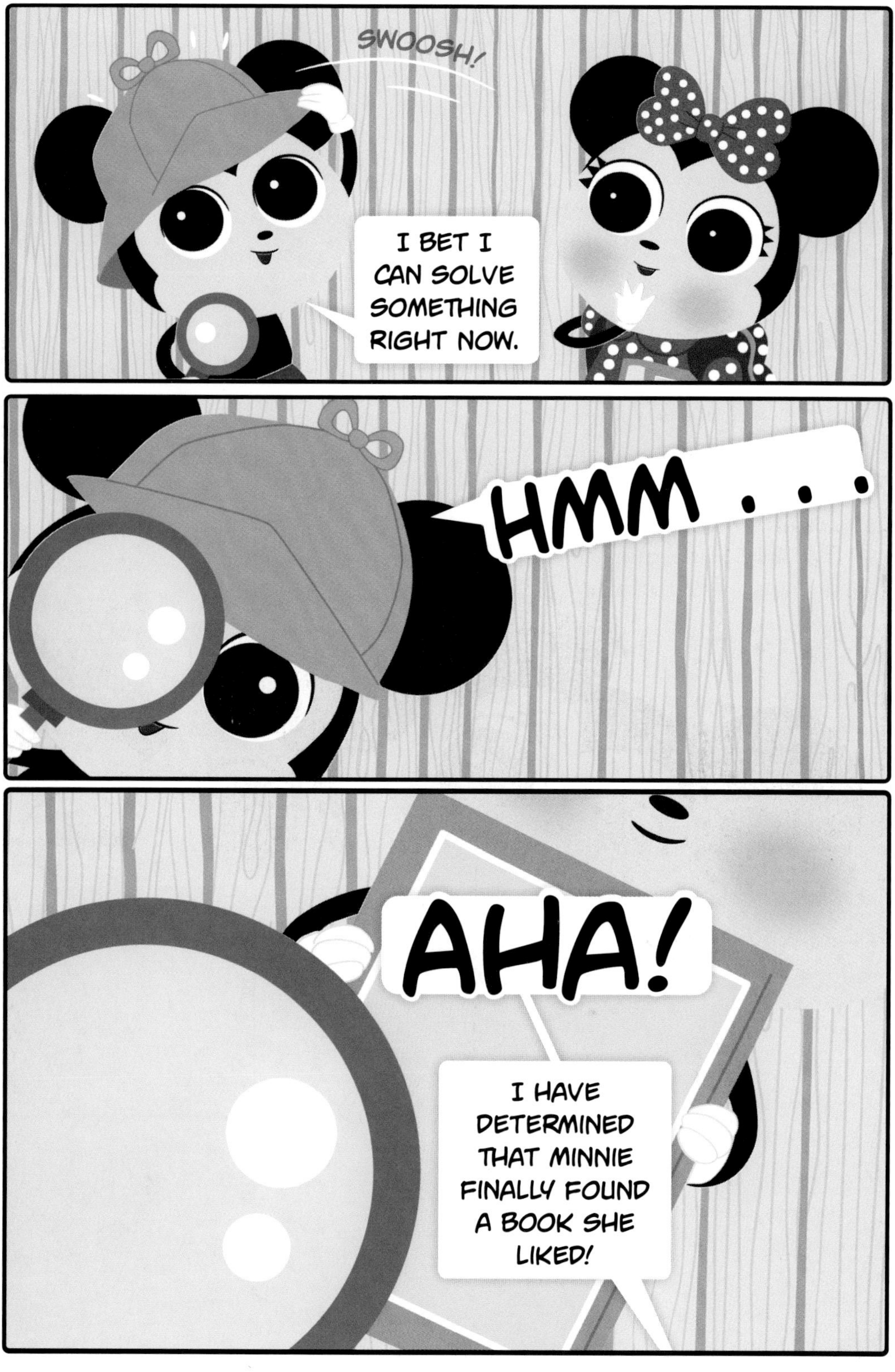
SWOOSH!
I BET I CAN SOLVE SOMETHING RIGHT NOW.
HMM . . .
AHA!
I HAVE DETERMINED THAT MINNIE FINALLY FOUND A BOOK SHE LIKED!

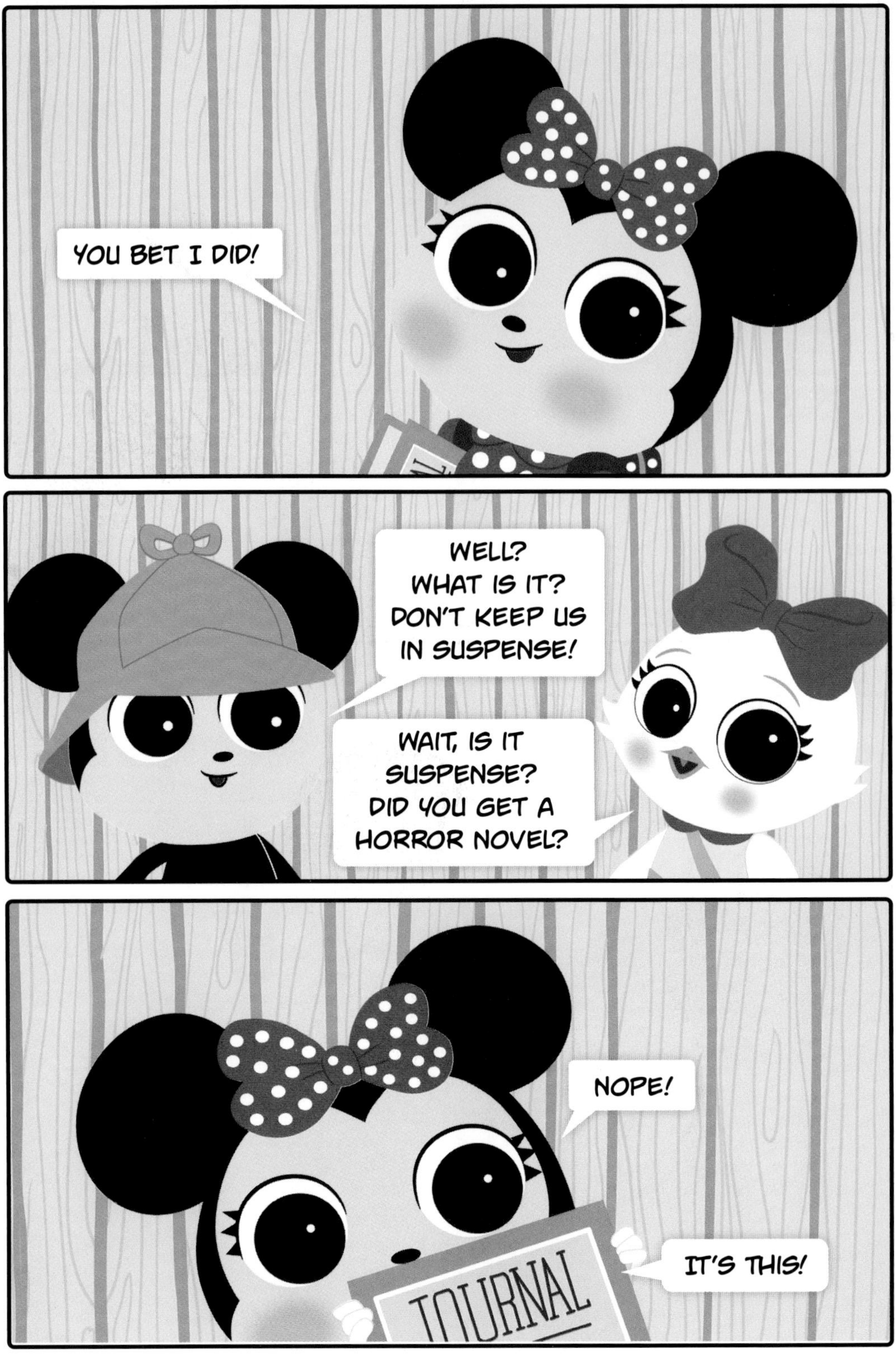
YOU BET I DID!
WELL? WHAT IS IT? DON'T KEEP US IN SUSPENSE!
WAIT, IS IT SUSPENSE? DID YOU GET A HORROR NOVEL?
NOPE!
IT'S THIS!
JOURNAL

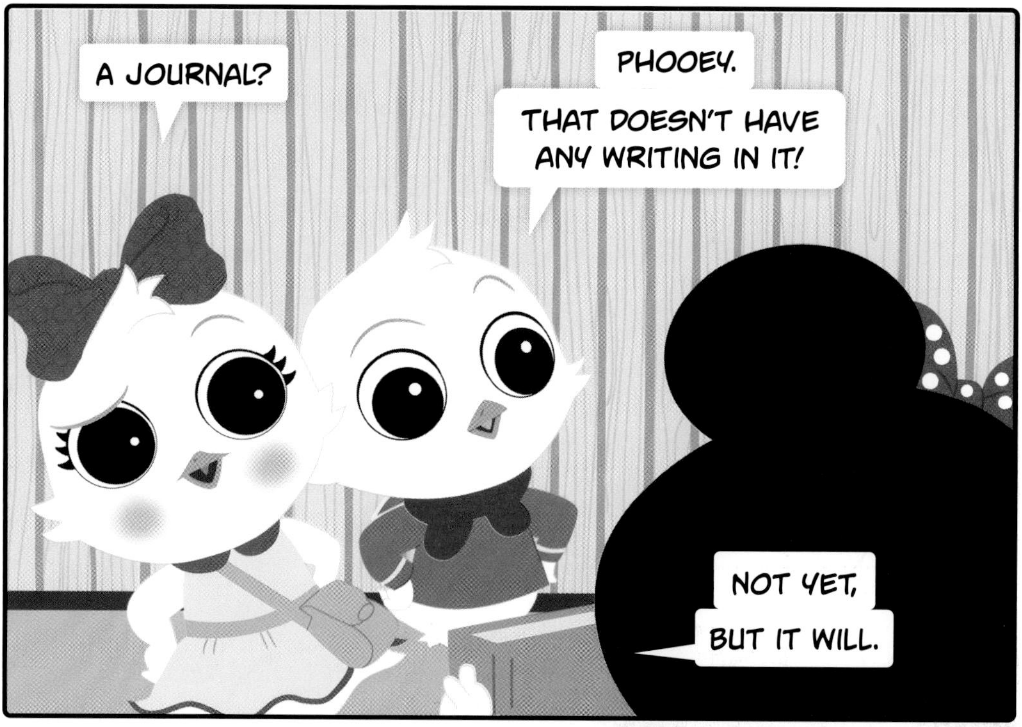
A JOURNAL?
PHOOEY.
THAT DOESN'T HAVE ANY WRITING IN IT!
NOT YET,
BUT IT WILL.

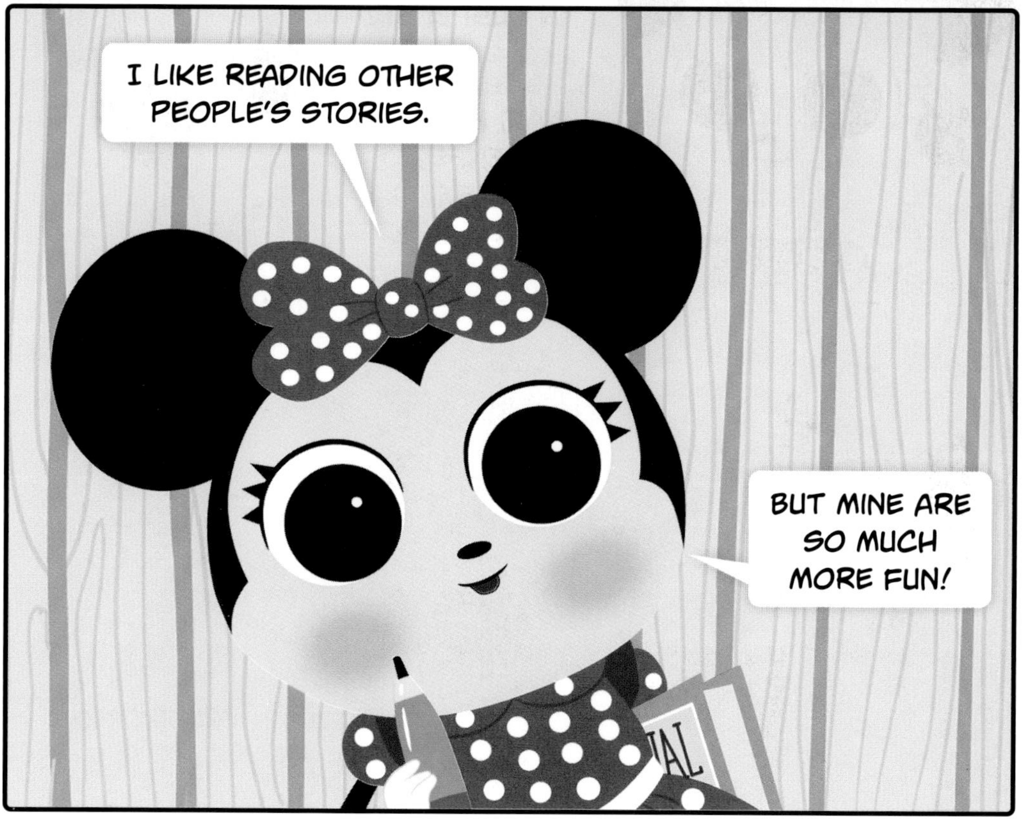
I LIKE READING OTHER PEOPLE'S STORIES.
BUT MINE ARE SO MUCH MORE FUN!

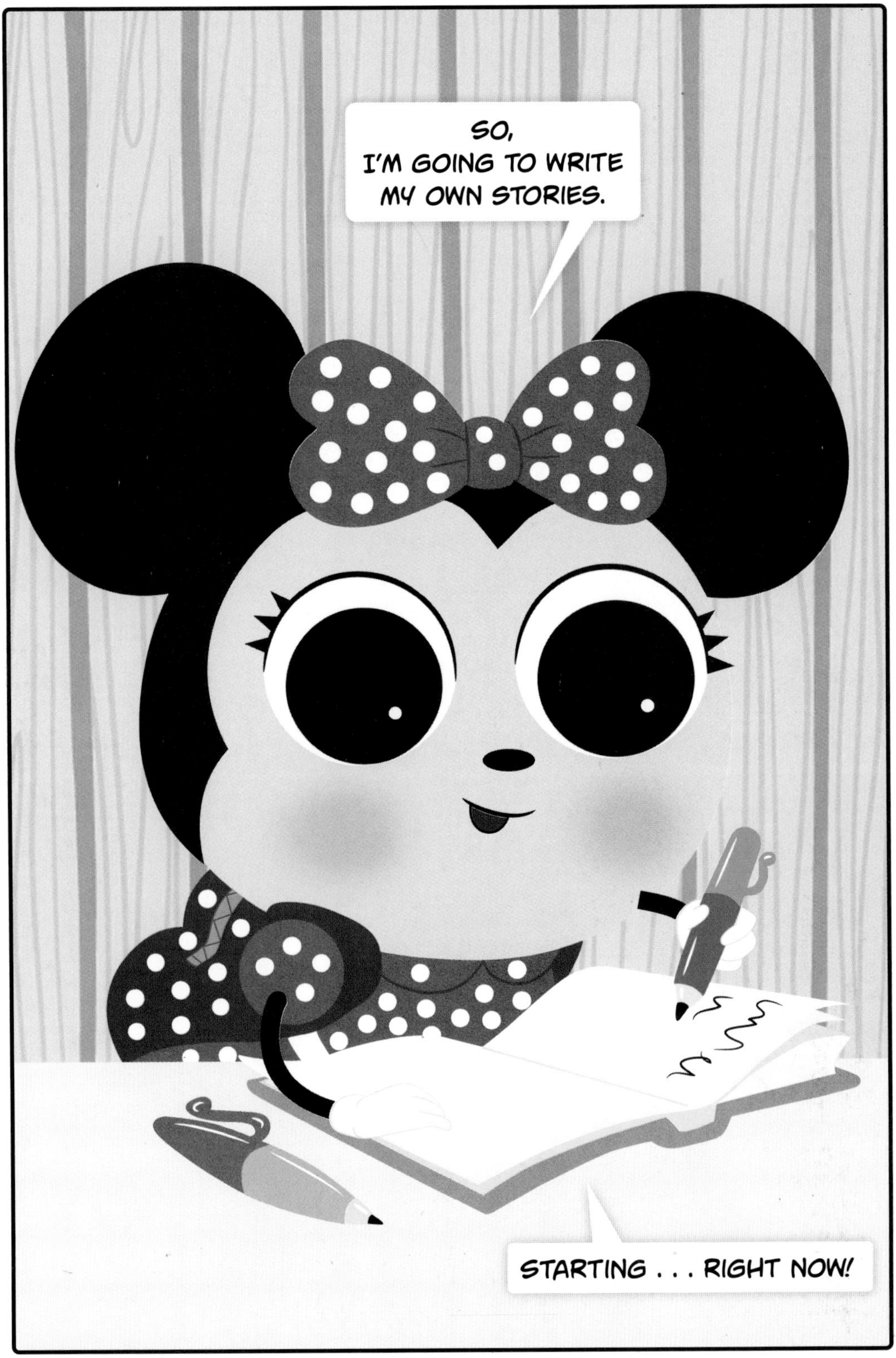
SO,
I'M GOING TO WRITE
MY OWN STORIES.
STARTING . . . RIGHT NOW!